lisa samson

Finding Hollywood Nobody

Book 2

a novel

For a free catalog
of NavPress books & Bible studies call
1-800-366-7788 (USA) or 1-800-839-4769 (Canada).

www.navpress.com

TH1NK
P.O. Box 35001
Colorado Springs, Colorado 80935

ISBN-10: 1-60006-201-6
ISBN-13: 978-1-60006-201-8

Cover design by The DesignWorks Group, David Uttley, www.thedesignworksgroup.com
Cover photo by PixelWorks Studios, Steve Gardner
Creative Team: Erin Healy, Darla Hightower, Arvid Wallen, Kathy Guist

This novel is a work of fiction. Names, characters, places, and incidents are either the product of the author's imagination or are used fictitiously. Any resemblance to actual events, locales, organizations, or persons, living or dead, is entirely coincidental and beyond the intent of either the author or publisher.

Published in association with the literary agency of Alive Communications, Inc., 7680 Goddard Street, Suite 200, Colorado Springs, CO 80920 (www.alivecommunications .com).

Library of Congress Cataloging-in-Publication Data
Samson, Lisa, 1964-
  Finding Hollywood nobody. Book 2 / Lisa Samson.
    p. cm.
  ISBN 978-1-60006-201-8 (alk. paper)
  1. Teenage girls--Fiction. 2. Parent and child--Fiction. 3. Family secrets--Fiction. 4. Texas--Fiction. I. Title.
PS3569.A46673F56 2007
813'.54--dc22

                        2007029793

Printed in the United States of America

1 2 3 4 5 6 7 8 9 10 / 12 11 10 09 08

Other Young Adult Books by Lisa Samson

Hollywood Nobody
Apples of Gold: A Parable of Purity

Dedication

For Ty
Thanks for the inspiration for Scotty!
I love seeing you change into
a wonderful young woman.
I love you,
Mom

Acknowledgments

Many thanks to:

Jeanne (critique friend), George, Luke, and Jacob Damoff, my hosts in Marshall, Texas! The ladies at the Design Center who showed us the old Elks Lodge and gave me my location for the shoot. Joe Buck and his coffee shop, which served as inspiration for Jacob and Luke's. Nathan Bach for time well spent, a mini-concert, and a fabulous CD.

Shanna, Randy, and Tesla Phoebe, the Tulsa contingent.

My daughter Gwynnie for accompanying me on the road trip to research for this book. Elvis Presley, the lady at Pirtle's Chicken, and Eero Saarinen — for ending our trip with form *and* function.

Ty, for reading all the drafts. Erin Healy, who told me what I needed to do to get it right and for being my partner of words and phrases on this journey of writing books. Kris and Arvid and the NavPress team!

And my new Hollywood Nobody reader friends! You all rock. I'm just sayin'!

E-mail me at lisa@lisasamson.com.

Hollywood Nobody: Sunday, June 4

Well, Nobodies, it's a wrap! Jeremy's latest film, yet another remake of *The Great Gatsby*, now titled *Green Light*, has shipped out from location and will be going into postproduction. Look for it next spring in theaters. It may just be his most widely distributed film yet with <u>Annette Bening</u> on board. Toledo Island will never be the same after that wacky bunch filled in their shores.

Today's Hottie Watch: Seth Haas has moved to Hollywood. An obscure film he did in college, *Catching Regina's Heels* (a five-star film in my opinion), was mentioned on the *Today* show last week. He was interviewed on NPR's *Fresh Air*. Hmm. Could it be he'll receive the widespread acclaim he deserves before the release of *Green Light*? For his sake and the film's, I hope so.

Rehab Alert: I've never hidden the fact that I don't care for bratty actress Karissa Bonano, but she just checked into rehab for a cocaine addiction. Her maternal grandfather, <u>Doug Fairmore</u>, famous in the forties for swashbuckling and digging up clues, made a <u>public statement</u> declaring the Royal Family of Hollywood was "indeed throwing all of our love, support, and prayers behind Karissa." The man must be a thousand years old by now. This isn't Ms. Bonano's first stint in rehab, but let's hope it's her last. Even I'm not too catty to wish her well in this battle. But I'm as skeptical as the next person. In Hollywood, rehab is mostly just a fad.

Today's Quote: "It's a scientific fact. For every year a person lives in Hollywood, they lose two points of their IQ." <u>Truman Capote</u>

Today's Rant: SWAG, or Party Favors. Folks, do you ever wonder what's inside those <u>SWAG bags</u> the stars get? Items which, if sold, could feed a third-world country for a week! And have you noticed how the people who can afford to buy this stuff seem to get it for free? I'm just sayin'. So here's my idea, stars: Refuse to take these high-priced bags 'o' stuff and gently suggest the advertisers give to a charitable organization on behalf of the movie, the stars, the whoever. Like you need another cell phone.

Today's Kudo: <u>Violette Dillinger</u> will be appearing on the MTV Video Music Awards in August. She told Hollywood Nobody she's going to prove to this crowd you can be young, elegant, decent, and still rock out. Go Violette!

Summer calls. Later!

Monday, September 15, 4:00 a.m.

Maybe I'm looking for the wrong thing in a parent.

I turn over in bed at the insistence of Charley's forefinger poking me in the shoulder. "Please tell me you've MapQuested this jaunt, Charley."

She shakes her tousled head, silhouetted by the yellow light emanating from the RV's bathroom. "You're kidding me right?" She slides off the dinette seat. Charley's been overflowing with relief since she told me the truth about our life: that she's not really my mother, but my grandmother, that somebody's chasing us for way too good of a reason, that my life isn't as boring as I thought. We're still being chased, but Charley can at least breathe more freely in her home on the road now that I know the truth.

Home in this case happens to be a brand-spanking-new Trailmaster RV, a huge step forward from the ancient Travco we used to have, the ancient Travco with a rainbow Charley spread in bright colors over its nose.

"Where to?" Having set my vintage cat glasses, love 'em, on my nose, I scramble my hair into its signature ponytail: messy, curly, and frightening. I can so picture myself in the *Thriller* video.

"Marshall, Texas."

"East Texas?"

"I guess."

"It is." I shake my head. Charley. I love her, I really do, but when it comes to geography, despite the fact that we've traveled all over the country going to her gigs ever since I can remember, she's about as intelligent as a bottle of mustard. And boy do I know a lot about bottles of mustard. But that was my last adventure.

"If you knew, then why did you ask?" She flips the left side of her long, blonde hair, straighter than Russell Crowe, over her shoulder. Charley's beautiful. Silvery blonde (she uses a cheap rinse to cover up the gray), thin (she's vegan), and a little airy (she's frightened of a lot and tries not to think about anything else that may scare her), she wears all sorts of embroidered vests and large skirts and painted blue jeans. And they're all the real deal, because Charley's an environmentalist and wouldn't dream of buying something she didn't need when what she's got is wearing perfectly well. She calls my penchant for vintage clothing "recycling," and I don't disagree.

"Is this really a gig, Charley, or are we escaping again?"

She shakes her head. "No phone call. I really do have a job."

I feel the thrill of fear inside me, though there's no need right now. Biker Guy almost got me back on Toledo Island. (Yeah, he looks like a grizzled old biker.) To call the guy rough around the edges would be like saying Pam Anderson has had "a little work done."

I've been looking over my shoulder ever since.

But more on that later. We need to get on the road. And I need to get on with my life. I'm so sick of thinking about how things aren't nearly what I'd like them to be.

I mean, do you ever get tired of hearing yourself complain?

I flip up my laptop, log on to the satellite Internet I installed (yes, I am that geeky) and Google directions to Marshall, Texas, from where we are in Theta, Tennessee—actually, on the farm of one of Charley's old art-school friends who gave her some work in advertising for the summer. Charley's a food stylist, which means she makes food look good for the camera. Still cameras, motion picture cameras, video, it doesn't matter. Charley can do it all.

"Oh, we've got plenty of time, Charley. Five hundred and fifty miles and . . . we have to go through Memphis . . ."

My verbal drop-off is a dead giveaway.

"Oh, no, Scotty, we're not going to Graceland again."

The kitsch that is Graceland speaks to me. What can I say?

And you've got to admit, it's starting to look vintage. Now ten years ago . . .

I cross my arms. "Do you have cooking to do on the way?"

Yes, highly illegal to cook in a rolling camper.

"Yeah, I do."

"And do you expect me, an unlicensed sixteen-year-old, to drive?" Again, highly illegal, but Charley's a free spirit. However, she refuses to copy CDs and DVDs, so in that regard, she's more moral than most people. I guess it evens up in the end.

"Uh-huh."

"Then I think I deserve a trip through the Jungle Room."

She rolls her eyes, reaches down to the floor, and throws me my robe. "Oh, all right. Just don't take too long."

"I'll try. So." I look at the screen. "65 to route 40 west. Let's hit it. And we'll have time to stop for breakfast."

Charley shakes her head and plops down on the tan dinette bench. The interior of this whole RV is a nice sandy tan with botanical accents. Tasteful and so much better than the old Travco that looked like a cross between a genie's bottle and the Unabomber cabin. "You're going to eat cheese. Aren't you?"

"I sure am."

And Charley can't say anything, because months ago she told me this was a decision I could make on my own.

Freedom!

"I've rethought the cheese moratorium, baby. I know you're not going to like this, but three months of cheese is enough. I can't imagine what your arteries look like. I think it's time to stop."

"What?" Cheese is my life. "Charley! You can't do this to me."

"It's for your own good."

"Are you serious?"

"Yeah, I am."

"Why?"

"Because summer's over, baby, and we've got to get back to a better way of life."

I could continue to argue, but it won't do any good. Charley acts all hippie and egalitarian, but when push comes to shove, she's the boss. However, I'm great at hiding my cheese . . . and . . . I'm going to convince her eventually.

But still.

"This isn't right, Charley, and you know it. But it's too early to argue. And might I add, you have no idea what it's like to have a teen with real teen issues. You ought to be on your knees thanking God I'm not drinking, smoking, pregnant, or" — I was going to say sneaking out at night, but I've done that, just to get some space — "or writing suicidal poetry on the Internet!"

We stare at each other, then burst into laughter.

"Just humor me this time, baby," she says. "We'll come back to it soon, I promise."

I don't believe her, but I hop into the driver's seat, push down the brake, throw the TrailMama into drive, and we are off.

Six hours later . . .

I pull through Graceland's gatehouse at ten a.m., park near the back of the compound's cracked, tired parking lot, and change into some crazy seventies striped bell-bottoms, a poet shirt, and Charley's old crocheted, granny-square vest. Normally I go further back in my vintage-wear, but I'm trying to go with the groove that is Graceland.

I kiss Charley's cheek. "I'll be back by noon."

"When will that put us in Marshall?"

"By six thirty."

"Because I'm not sure where the shoot is."

"Please. Marshall's small. Jeremy and company will make a big splash no matter where they set up. Besides, growing up around this, I have a nose for it."

She awards me one of her big smiles. "You're somethin', baby. I forget that sometimes." She puts her arms around me, squeezes, pulls back, then smacks me lightly on my behind. "Tell Elvis I said hello."

"Oh, I will. He's one of the groundskeepers now, you know."

I've seen computer-generated pictures of what he would look like now, in his seventies. Scary.

I jump down from the RV, head across the parking lot, over the small bridge leading into the ticketing complex and walk by Elvis's jets, including the *Lisa Marie*. Gotta love anything with that name. Don't know why. Just has a nice ring to it.

Banners proclaim, "Elvis Is."

Is what? Dead? A legend? What? Because he isn't "izzing" as far as I'm concerned. Present tense, people! If the person's not alive, "is" can only be followed by a few options: Buried up in the memorial garden. Rotting in his casket. Missed by his family and friends. Not exactly banner copy, mind you.

Still, you've got to admit the name Elvis reeks of cool. Perhaps the sign should read, "Elvis Is . . . A Really Cool Name."

But it's not nearly as cool as my name. You see, my real mother loved the writer F. Scott Fitzgerald. And that's my name: Francis Scott Fitzgerald Dawn. Only Dawn's not my actual last name. I don't know what my real last name is. My real first name is Ariana. Being on the run, Charley renamed us to protect our identity. So she honored my mother by naming me after Mom's favorite novelist. More on that later too.

It sounds fun, traveling on the road from film shoot to film shoot, never settling down in one place for too long, but honestly, it's very sad.

I always knew Charley lived with a sadness down deep, and when I found out why this spring, her sadness became mine. See, my dad is dead and my mother, Charley's daughter Babette, is too. Or we think she must be, because she disappeared under questionable circumstances and never came back. Learn that when you're fifteen and see where you land.

When I thought Charley was my mother, I had such high hopes for who my father might be. Al Pacino was number one in the ranking. Don't ask.

Okay, Elvis, here we go. Let's you and me be "taking care of business."

I hand over my money to the lady behind the reservations counter. I called thirty minutes ago on my cell phone, compliments of my mother's friend Jeremy, and reserved a spot.

"You'll be on the first tour."

Yes! More time amid the shag carpeting and the gold records. And the jumpsuits. Can't forget the jumpsuits. I want a cape too.

The gift shop calls to me. Confession: I love gift shops. They even smell sparkly. Key chains dangling, saying, "You can take me with you wherever you go!" Mugs with the Saint Louis Gateway Arch or the Grand Ole Opry promising an even better cup of coffee. Earrings that advertise you've been somewhere. That's exactly what I choose while I wait for the tour, a little pair of dangly red guitars with the words Elvis Presley in gold script on the bodies, and how in the world they put that on so small is beyond me. See, gift shops can even be miraculous if you take your time and look.

A voice over the loudspeaker announces my tour number, so I stand in line. By myself. Just me in a group of twenty or so.

Okay, here is where it gets hard to be me. I know I should be thankful for my free-spirited life. But especially now that I know my parents are dead, it feels empty all of a sudden. I shouldn't be standing in line at Graceland alone. My mother and I should be giggling behind our hands at the man nearby who's actually grown a glorious pair o' mutton-chop sideburns, slicked back his salt-and-pepper curls, and shrugged his broad shoulders into a leather jacket. Really, right? My father, who was an FBI agent the mob shot right in a warehouse in Baltimore, would shake his head like a dad in a sixties TV show and laugh at his girls.

We'd get on the bus like I'm doing now, each of us putting on our tour headphones and hanging the little blue recorders around our necks in anticipation of the glory that is Elvis.

The driver welcomes us as he shuts the hydraulic doors of the small tour bus with its clean blue upholstery, a bus in which an assisted-living home might haul its residents to the mall.

It smells new in here, and my gross-out antennae aren't vibrating in the least like they do when I go into an old burger joint and the orange melamine booth hasn't been scrubbed since the place opened in 1987.

In my fantasy, my dad would sit beside me. And Mom, just across the aisle, holding onto the seatback in front of her, would look at me as we pass through those famed musical gates, because she would have introduced me to Elvis music. According to Charley, my vintage sentimentalism comes from my mom. I've learned a little about her this summer.

Charley said, "She'd wear my cousin's old poodle skirt and listen to *Love Me Tender* over and over again while writing in her diary." She became a respected journalist, loved books as much as I do. I pat my book in my backpack, looking forward to tonight when I can cuddle into my loft and get into one of Fitzgerald's glittering worlds. "She was different from me, Scotty. I tried to change the world through protest. Your mother wanted to build something completely different and much better." She sighed. "All my generation could do, I guess, was tear apart. It's going to take our children to put the pieces back together. Babette was a very careful person. Very purposeful."

If it drove my freewheeling grandmother crazy, she doesn't let on.

"I could try to describe how much she loved you, baby. But I don't think I could begin to do her devotion to you justice. I was so proud of her, for how much she loved and gave away. She was amazing."

So in May I found out she existed, the same day I found out she is dead, or most likely dead. And now I'm going into Graceland alone, truly an orphan. Who wants to be an orphan?

We disembark from the bus—me, Elvis Lite, some folks from a Spanish-speaking country, and a lot of older people. I miss Grammie and Grampie right now. More later on them, too. And you'll get to meet them. Like the waters of the Gulf Stream, we seem to travel in the same general direction. I spent a week with them this summer in Tennessee. Yeah, we did Nashville right. They're loaded.

Standing beneath the front porch, my gaze skates up and down the soaring white pillars and comes to rest on the stone lions that guard the steps. My father was a lion. That's why he ended up with a bullet in his chest. Speaking in very broad terms, the story goes as follows:

Dad, undercover, worked his way into a portion of the mob, or mafia if you prefer, that was heavily financing the campaign of a Maryland gubernatorial candidate. When they discovered him, they shot him on site, in a warehouse in the Canton neighborhood of downtown Baltimore. My mother watched, gasped, and a chase ensued. She hid in a friend's gallery, called Charley and told her to keep watching me. (Charley had kept me the night before because my mom and dad had some glamorous function to attend.) And then she disappeared.

The Graceland tour recorder tells me to look to my right into the beautiful white living room with peacock stained-glass windows leading into the music room. This room really isn't so bad, I've got to admit. A picture of Elvis's dad hangs on the wall. He really loved his parents.

I've toured this house at least seven times before, and I'll tell you this, Elvis's love for his family soaked into the walls. A girl that lives in a camper, has dead parents, and is being chased by someone from the mob who knows my grandmother knows what went down, well, she can feel these things.

Charley thinks someone's trying to kill us. This guy is always trying to find us, but Charley's really great at evasion. She said the politician who won the governor's seat all those years ago just announced his candidacy for president and — oh, GREAT! — he's probably trying to make sure nothing comes back to haunt him and sent Biker Guy to finish off the entire matter.

The thing is, he seems to be after me too. And what in the world would I have to do with all of that?

I'll bet Charley's back in that camper shaking in her shoes because I'm over here by myself; I'll bet she's figuring out more ways to be utterly and overly protective of me. I wouldn't be surprised if she's wondering whether locking a kid in an RV is child abuse.

But I love Charley. I really do. I know she's scared back there, and despite the fact that I would be no real help if Biker Guy caught us, I can't leave her there so frightened and alone for long.

Elvis dear, I can only stay a little while. So love me tender, love me sweet, and for the sake of all that's decent, don't step on my blue suede shoes.

I hurry past the bedroom of Elvis's parents, decorated in shades of ivory and purple, very nice, and through the dining room—a little seventies tackiness I'll admit—into the kitchen with dark brown cabinetry and the ghosts of a million grilled peanut butter and banana sandwiches, then on down into the basement. Okay, I admit, I've got to just stand for a second in the TV room and admire the man's ability to watch three TVs at once on that huge yellow couch with the sparkly pillows.

I shoot through the billiard room, which is, honestly, truly beautiful with its fabric-lined walls and ceiling, up the back steps and into the Jungle Room, probably Graceland's most famous room. Green shag carpet overlays the floor and the ceiling, and heavily carved, Polynesian-style furniture is arranged around a rock-wall waterfall at the end of the room. It really defies the imagination, folks. Google *Jungle Room Graceland* and see what I mean.

The second floor of Graceland is closed off to the public because Elvis died up there. On the toilet. Wise decision on the part of Priscilla I'd say.

Out the door, into the office building, down to the trophy hall, I whiz through all the gold and platinum records, the costumes, the awards, and even a wall full of checks he'd written for charity. According to my recorder, Elvis was an active community member in Memphis. And he obviously didn't care what race or religion people were. He supported Jewish organizations, Catholic, Baptist. Pretty cool.

Of course, this recorder isn't going to tell of the dark side of the man. But Elvis Isn't, despite what the banners say. So why drag a dead man through the mud?

I hurry through the racquetball court, more gold records, the infamous jumpsuits, back outside to the pool and memorial garden where Elvis has been laid to rest.

An older lady cries into a handkerchief. I don't ask why.

Good-bye Elvis. Thanks for the tour. Maybe one day I'll do something great too.

A few minutes later . . .

Charley waves me down across the parking lot. Oh, no. She's received one of her mysterious phone calls, I'll bet.

"Hurry, baby!"

"Okay!" I pick up to a run, practically skidding into her. "You get a call?"

"Yeah. He's headed our way. Hop in."

I jump up into the RV and turn to face her. "I wish we knew who warned us all the time."

"Me too. First of all, how do they even know my cell phone number? It's all under Jeremy's name. And how do they know where that man is?"

I shake my head. "I have no idea." I've tried to track the number from her caller ID, but it's always blocked.

"I know they're on our side. At least there's that." Charley takes the wheel. "I really thought the new RV would throw him off for longer than a few months."

"Me too."

I buckle in beside her. "Guess it's hard to keep two hot babes like us anonymous for long."

Charley laughs. "That's a good attitude, baby."

"I mean, it is what it is, and we can't change it unless we go to the cops."

"Oh, we can't go to the cops!"

"Why not?"

She pulls forward and circles the lot. "They can be as bad as anybody else. The one I dated said he'd kill me if he ever saw me again."

"Are you kidding me?"

"I wish I was." We slide by the gatehouse.

"Well at least it wasn't murder or anything. Right? You haven't killed anybody have you, Charley?"

"No, baby. I haven't. And that's the truth."

I really can't believe a word my grandmother says, but for some reason, I know she's shooting straight with me on this one. Or at least I think so.

We continue toward Marshall, Texas, hopefully way ahead of the man who seeks to hurt us.

"Charley, how long has it been since he's been stalking us?"

"Several years. The good governor started hinting around at running for president around that time too."

"Whoa."

"Yeah, so I'm thinking they're trying to make sure nothing's going to pop up to damage his chances at winning."

"That's my theory too. Do you think this guy could be after you about the counterfeiting?"

"No. There are a lot bigger fish to fry than me. It wasn't a huge amount, and I wasn't a big threat, but it's enough to land me in jail and enough to keep me flying under the radar."

She turns onto Elvis Presley Boulevard.

"You should have gone left."

"I know. But let's find you something to eat."

"What if you go to the candidate and tell him you won't make any trouble?"

She just turns her head and stares at me.

"I know." I sigh. "I realized how dumb that was as soon as it left my mouth. Maybe he'll have a massive heart attack or a stroke or something, be rendered unfit to run for office, and then we'd be safe."

Charley laughs. "That sure would be nice."

A few minutes later we pull into Pirtle's Chicken.

"Chicken? Really?" I almost gush.

"Sure, go ahead up to the window and order. I'll just heat myself up some leftover beans."

She pulls around to the side of the lot and I hop out.

"Nothing with cheese!" she calls after me.

The primary-colored building emits the smell of fried chicken. The sign promises "home-cooked taste." I'm ready to swoon from the aroma alone and the thought of crispy skin and juicy meat? Well, somebody catch me!

An elderly African American woman behind the counter calls me sugar, and I want to ask if she'll be my aunt. Her eyes, set deep in the folds of her velvet skin, sparkle with a rascally wisdom; her voice resonates, alto musical.

"I'd like the three-piece, dark meat special."

"Potatoes with that?" She turns toward the warming table.

"Oh, yes!"

"That your RV?" she calls over her shoulder as she places the chicken pieces, two thighs and . . . oh, two legs, and obviously she's taking pity on me by giving me the extra piece.

"Yes ma'am."

"Nice one. Shouldn't you be in school?"

"I'm homeschooled." There it is. My face reddens with embarrassment. "My grandmother's job keeps us on the road."

"You bein' raised by your grandmother?"

"Yes, ma'am."

"So was I." She smiles at me for the first time. "You seem to be doing all right. Brothers and sisters?"

"Just me."

"You lonely then."

I nod.

"Well this chicken's made with love. You enjoy it."

I look into her eyes. She's loving me and I don't understand it, but it's like the rays of the sun shine through her.

Four hours later . . .

Farther on down the road, my cell phone rings. "It's Grammie and Grampie."

26

Charley shakes her head. Any incoming call seems so risky. "All right." Sigh.

"Hello?"

"Hi, Scotty."

"Grampie!"

"Where are you?"

"I just went to Graceland."

"Us too. Billie Jo loves that Elvis."

"Oh, George!" I can hear her in the background.

"Where are you guys headed?" I ask.

Charley pulls off into a rest area.

"We're not sure. Where are you going?"

"Marshall, Texas."

"Hmm. Have you researched it yet?"

What can I say? Grampie knows me.

"A little, while I ate my chicken. Grew with the railroad, has some cool historical buildings left. Jeremy's shooting a horror picture for that pet project of his."

"Is that right? Well, would you mind if we tag along?"

"Hang on." I hop up from my seat. Charley's in the back of the RV. "Charley, is it okay if Grammie and Grampie hang around Marshall with us?"

"I don't know, baby. It might be dangerous for them with that man so close on our tracks."

"Hey, they were there for me in North Carolina. They know the risks."

"We sure do!" Grampie's voice calls from the phone I'm now holding down at my waist.

"I guess it's okay."

I lift the phone back to my ear. "Come on down!"

"You tell Charley we appreciate it. We'll pull in sometime tomorrow afternoon. We've already settled for the night near Hot Springs."

"What park?"

"Cloud Nine."

"That's a nice one."

After we say good-bye, Charley opens the curtain to her cubicle, dressed in nice jeans and a cotton blouse she embroidered this summer.

"Wow, you look beautiful, Charley."

"Thanks."

She loves Jeremy, the film director we do a lot of work for. I suspected it before, but now I know it for sure. She's fancied herself up like she hasn't done in months.

And I'm so going to get those two together. Wait and see.

Hollywood Nobody: Monday, September 15

Hello, fellow Nobodies! Little Me has hit the road and will have tales to tell, I'm sure, from location. There's rumor that Karissa Bonano will be on set. Stay tuned for more ludicrous, tragic, and thoroughly predictable antics. Supposedly, heartbroken by Seth "Hottie" Haas, she spent a good part of the summer, after rehab, in London. But she's back with a vengeance, partying up the night. So much for rehab.

Today's Kudo: Julia Roberts. Did you know she doesn't have a nanny to help her with Hazel, Phinnaeus, and Henry? Good for her! Which leads me to . . .

Today's Rant: With those names, except Henry of course, those tots will need more help than any nanny could provide. What are some of these stars thinking with these names? *What?* Apple? Rumer? Scout? Moxie *Crime*fighter? Despite what these parents are thinking, their own popularity won't carry their children into coolness and acceptance.

Today's News: Violette Dillinger is following up her rockin' performance on the MTV Video Music Awards by continuing her tour to sold-out audiences. So far she's keeping her head on straight. Last week Violette, who has made Hollywood Nobody her exclusive site for personal news ("The Britney blogging stuff is so yesterday," she says. "And the Nobodies are my kind of people.") told me she's signed up for the OpenCourseWare at MIT. (That's Massachusetts Institute of Technology, folks! A place for really smart people!) "I'm on the road a lot. I love school. I need to keep learning. I mean, don't we all?" Go, Violette.

Seth "Hottie" Haas News: The cutest new young star is filming alongside Brad Pitt and Susan Sarandon in a coming-of-age film as yet untitled, but based on the novel *Tiny Shards of Light* by a Sudanese refugee who simply calls herself Rage. What white people like that are doing in a coming-of-age story written by somebody from the Sudan is something I wouldn't have figured out on my own until I read this article on Rage, who said: "It's an American film. The principles are timeless. I wanted as many people who will see it to relate to my story." So there you have it.

Today's Quote: "I love Los Angeles. I love Hollywood. They're beautiful. Everybody's plastic, but I love plastic. I want to be plastic." Andy Warhol

Speaking of plastic, did you see what's happened to <u>Vivica A. Fox</u>? Oh, my. I used to think she was the most beautiful woman out there. Too bad she didn't think so too.

Later!

Tuesday, September 16, 8:00 a.m.

We found the film crew easily last night. Trailers and trucks took up breathing space in the parking lots lining Wellington Street. This is a smaller shoot because it's Jeremy's pet project.

Okay, so he's been working on this project for over a decade, shooting footage once a year, and nobody can figure out how in the world it will someday come together. It's pretty crazy.

And yes, this fits into the horror genre, quite possibly my least favorite of all. With Karissa Bonano playing the female lead, I'd say that it all works together. She does have the best scream in the business. I have to give her that.

I jump down from the TrailMama and head over to Jeremy's Airstream at the edge of camp. Jeremy's owned this tin can on wheels for years. Inside he sleeps on a couch covered in leopard prints. I'm sure he just takes off his cowboy boots, sets his hat on that asymmetrical triangular coffee table, lays his weary, older-guy body on the couch, and snores the night away.

The trailer door's open.

"Jeremy?" I peek my head in.

"Come on in, kiddo."

Back in the day when I had no idea who my father was, I used to dream Jeremy sired me. I know better now, and I still love him just as much, even though he can be downright ornery and aloof sometime. Artists, you know.

I climb in. "What are you cooking? Smells good."

"A western, want one?"

"Yeah, boy."

"Sit down. Nice pants."

Powder-blue pedal pushers, vintage 1962. "Yeah, they go with the cat glasses, don't you think?"

He laughs and cracks an egg into a pan.

Jeremy makes western sandwiches: hamburger, a fried egg, relish, and cheese on a grilled bun. Don't knock it until you've tried it is all I've got to say. Charley's busy. She'll never find out about the cheese.

"So why Karissa Bonano, Jeremy?"

In case you haven't gotten it, the chick is my nemesis. She was really snobby to me at our last shoot, and Seth Haas—yes, the upcoming Hollywood hottie who's become one of my best friends—actually fell for her, which just goes to show you that even the smartest people do stupid things.

Jeremy laughs as he removes the burgers from the cast-iron skillet and lays down two open buns on their faces. "You really don't like her, do you?" He flips the eggs over. "I'm finding her to be quite the muse."

A muse? Oh, I feel like hurling. "I don't like her at all. Jeremy, she was doing cocaine on your last shoot. Why take a chance?"

He arranges a spoonful of relish on each patty. "She's clean. I'm relatively sure."

"You're way more trusting than I am."

He slaps some cheese atop the burgers. "Look, kid, she's the perfect actress for this piece."

"A horror piece," I grumble.

He arranges the masterpieces on the grilled buns and sets it all on plates. "Exactly. Some chips?"

"Oh yeah. But why horror, Jeremy? I hate horror movies."

"Look, the project has a little piece of everything. There's a horror portion, a romance portion, an action portion, a psychological thriller portion. The trick is going to be to make the story cohesive and seamless despite that."

"Good luck. And Karissa will probably ruin it for you."

"Thanks for that vote of confidence in my vision, kid."

"You're welcome."

"You keep me humble."

"I'm good at that."

He reaches up into the cupboard. "You know, kiddo, you just got to let it go about these actresses. They are who they are, they do what they do, and they're pretty much always gonna be this way. I'm still not sure why it bugs you so much or why you let it affect you the way you do."

I grunt.

Sitting down at the dinette, he slides a plate before me.

"Are you going to be as out of sorts as you were at the last shoot?" I ask. "I mean, 'Oh grand poo-bah!' I couldn't hardly come near you."

He takes a bite. I take a bite. And oh, the meat. Oh, the cheese. I chew and chew, the egg flavoring it all just right. Jeremy's not afraid to use a little pepper either.

"Tell you what, Scotty. If you need me, I'll be at the ready."

"You got it."

"Satisfied?"

"Uh-huh. Now stop distracting me from this sandwich."

Jeremy laughs. "Only you, kid. Only you. Oh, and Cillian Murphy is the male lead."

Cillian Murphy? Oh, man, I love Cillian Murphy.

But still.

The Karissa is coming. In fact, she may already be here.

I need a cup of coffee. Because as sure as Charley will eat soy products, I'll be running into that girl. Sooner than I'd like. 'Cause what *I'd* like is . . . *never*.

Thirty minutes later . . .

I head over to Ms. Burrell's, the costume mistress's trailer. She's already pushing fabric so fast through her industrial machine I have to shut my mouth. I know enough about Ms. Burrell, feisty, assured, and the color of cocoa powder, to wait until she looks up at me.

After a minute she does. "Well, Scotty, my baby! Come here and give your favorite person a hug."

Mmm. Ms. Burrell's figure could be described as *heroic*. All I know is, I love to be enfolded in her big warm arms. She smells like coconut, which matches her hair, bleached and lying in short, cream-colored quills around her head.

I pull back. "Karissa Bonano."

"Baby, I *know*! I said to Jeremy, 'That sweat box? *Again?*' And, of course, he just laughed. This is some piece, Scotty . . . you read the script yet?"

"No. I think Charley hides them from me because she knows how mad they always make me."

"Well, *I* know. But this one is actually pretty good. It's about this girl lost in an old hotel, and she goes crazy because all around her are the excesses of life, and baby, she's going to try it all."

Sounds like Nicole and Dick Diver, the main couple in my latest Fitzgerald read, *Tender Is the Night*. Only it wasn't a hotel, it was the French Riviera. I open a nearby folding chair and set it up next to her worktable. "So what's the hitch?"

"With each thing she tries, she loses a little bit of herself."

"Like, literally?"

"Uh-huh. Wakes up one morning without a pinkie and so forth from then on out."

"Ewww!"

"You got that right."

"She must be pretty stupid." Again, like Dick Diver in *Tender*. Talk about an idiot. To sacrifice so much for that crazy Nicole? What's wrong with the man?

"Which is why Jeremy got Karissa Bonano—hah-haaaah!"

True 'dat. Or whatever it is people who are a lot cooler than I am say. I'm not good at cool-speak. Not even close. I prefer to think of myself as "the intelligent type above all that."

My cell phone buzzes.

Ms. Burrell rolls her liquid brown eyes. "Oh, go ahead. You all and your phones!"

A text. Oh, cool. Sue me, but I love text messaging.

It's from Seth!

Seth: Where r u?

Me: In Texas.

Seth: Y?

Me: Jeremy's pet project. Where are you?

Seth: Going 2 the set. brd pitt awaits. ha!

Me: Is he nice?

Seth: Yeah. lks a lot oldr in prson.

Me: I'll bet. How much longer on the set?

Seth: A few days, thn we go on lcation to vermnt.

Me: Cool.

Seth: I may stp by tx on the way. ill hve a few days off.

Me: Very cool. Let me know when.

Seth: Ok. cu!

Me: Backatcha.

I shut my phone. Seth is a minimalist text messager. And I don't think he knows how to work the shift key for capital letters, but that's okay. I'll bet he doesn't know the Karissa is down here. Hmm. This should be interesting, him coming to see me while Karissa has to stand on the sidelines and watch!

I like it.

"So who was that?" Ms. Burrell reaches behind her and grabs a bolt of lavender chiffon.

"Seth Haas."

"Oh, I love that boy. How's he doing?"

"Fine. He's playing alongside Brad Pitt."

"You're not serious!"

"Yes."

"I'm not surprised. I been around these parts for a long time and I know who's got it, and that boy's got it."

"If he can stay away from Karissa Bonano. He's coming to visit for a couple of days. She'll be here. You know what I'm saying?"

She shakes her head. "I've seen young men do stupider things."

She leans forward and whispers, "You think she'll get him in her clutches again?"

The hair on the back of my neck stands up. "No. He's smarter than that, right?"

And Ms. Burrell laughs and laughs.

A few hours later . . .

So I fixed Charley and me a little lunch while she shopped for fresh produce. They're shooting the gluttony scene, so there has to be great-looking food all over the place. She's been to all the restaurants arranging deliveries for food because there's no way she'll be able to do all that on her own. It's going to be one heck of a day and I have my doubts whether the Karissa will be able to do anything with less than twenty takes.

But let's hope it doesn't take too long or all that food will spoil. This stuff is actually edible, unlike some of the uncooked turkeys bewitched to a golden brown with a blow torch and some Kitchen Bouquet. The crew could have a nice dinner if the Karissa will do her job like she's supposed to. If she's not high or drunk.

Do you know she has a really nice set of parents?

If that's not irony, I don't know what is.

I met them once years ago. Her dad's an actor and didn't mind when I sat in his chair. Then again, she divorced them when she was sixteen.

But it's time to get going on this year's schoolwork. I took the summer off completely, lounged around online with my blog and the other Hollywood rags, ate a lot of cheese, and actually found a few online high schools that will extend me credit and a diploma. I'm pretty behind in "real" classes, but I figure, give me two years and I'll have all the minimum requirements. I'm officially a student of Indiana University High School, which sounds cool anyway.

However, seeing as we move from place to place, I consider myself a traveling historian as well. During the drive here yesterday, I checked out Marshall and figure the best place to begin is the Ginocchio Hotel.

I grab my scooter, a little Razor-esque job with a motor and a seat, buzz out to Washington Street and take a left heading northward. Ooh, there's a little second-hand shop. Will definitely try that out. And the Design Center, which looks way too high-class for me. But they've got this freight elevator, and the crew is using it to get lighting and cameras up to second and third floors of the building next door where the shoot is taking place. Supposedly it's the old Elks Lodge.

Oh, shoot. My curiosity gets the better of me, so I zip up to the Design Center and secure my scooter to a light pole. When I walk in, a women strolls right up, dirty blonde, short hair, wrinkly eyes behind sleek red glasses, and a wide smile bordered by bright red lips. "We've got some cider samples in the back and some delicious spreads if you'd like some while you're browsing."

"Cream cheese spreads?"

"Yes, they're wonderful."

"Show me the way."

She leads me through the store housed in this old building. Carved pillars and a fancy mezzanine surround the room beneath a gold leaf ceiling. Polished wooden floors clonk beneath my kitten-heel slides.

There it is, the freight elevator, but I've got cheese on my mind. The sales clerk pours me a cup of hot cider—so autumny and I'm lovin' that—and I eat as many crackers as I can get away with without being rude.

But I came for a history lesson, and as I look around at the beautiful building, I wonder what it was used for back in the day.

"A car dealership," my lady tells me.

"No kidding."

She shows me a small area separated by waist-high walls and an iron grate surrounding its dimensions, making it something like a cage. Inside are a couple of desks and computers and a big adding machine. "This was the office area."

"Very cool."

She crosses her arms, very freckly arms attached to hands that look like they've made many a cookie for many a neighborhood kid. "You're not from Marshall, are you?"

"No. I'm here with the shoot."

Her brows rise. "How old are you?"

"Sixteen."

She cocks her head and I rush into an explanation. "My grandmother's the food stylist."

"You sure you're not one of those famous teen stars women my age have never heard of?"

"Oh, yeah. Definitely not one of those."

"By the way, I'm Dee."

"I'm Scotty." And we have the typical conversation as to why I have a boy's name.

She makes me up another cracker. "While you're here, let me

pick your brain. Kathy Ann has an idea for a film."

Now, normally my hackles would rise, but Dee is one of those people you'd invite off the street for a glass of limeade.

I listen as she tells me the idea, which is pretty much *Ya-Ya Sisterhood* in Texas. Old news. But in-between the scenes she thinks Hollywood will love, her eyes sparkle and the young woman comes out and I wish to goodness I could have been there with her and her big-haired friends in that old pickup truck as they busted their way toward Shreveport to go to the movies.

Apparently, in those days Dee went to a Free Will Baptist church that, "Expected you to take that free will and choose to do absolutely nothing with it."

She goes over to the Methodists now.

Methodism. John Wesley. And he's the man.

"So where do you go for a good cup of coffee in Marshall?" I slip the straps of my backpack over my shoulder.

"Well, depends on the atmosphere you want. Across the street at Weisman's it's bright and got a lot of bustle. But Jacob and Luke's Coffee over on Alamo is trendy and it's where a lot of the young people gather."

"How do I get there?"

She gives me directions and I head on up to the shoot, but they're all busy. Charley waves me over from a spot near the elevator. "Don't go into the Elks area. They're filming and Jeremy's in a mood." She gives me a little good-bye wave and gets back to arranging a platter of citrus fruit she brushed with corn oil earlier. One slips out of her hand and onto the floor.

And suddenly I feel so sad for her. She leans over, so vulnerable and at the mercy of fate.

Does my mother look like Charley? Was she a little ditzy,

prone to hold onto her good looks, smiley, and enjoying the wind in her hair?

She was a journalist. A person of words. Somewhat like me, I guess. What would she have thought of me now? Who would I have become had she been raising me? Charley said she was crazy about me.

Charley's crazy about me. But it's just not the same.

Is it?

Fifteen minutes later . . .

We're well into mid-September and all I've done school-wise is read F. Scott Fitzgerald. Of course. The fact that the blistering sun has no idea autumn is here does nothing to put me in the mood for schoolwork. But the last thing I need is for Charley to start checking up on me. So I putter down the hill toward the Ginocchio Hotel.

I mean, what else is there to do really?

Just shy of the hotel, a teenager stalks up the cement steps of an old stone house. She falls. Her cry sends me up to the curb and I jump off the scooter, fling my backpack down and hurry up the steps to where she sits.

She looks up at me, tears and anger streaking her made-up face. She's pretty in a sad, wistful way, rounded cheeks and deep blue eyes paring the sunlight to a minimum with a squint. "I knew I was taking those too fast. Darn it, I'm so clumsy!"

"It's okay." I sit down on the steps just below her. "These old steps can be so steep, and people were shorter back then than they are now. It makes no sense whatsoever. But it is what it is, right? Are you okay?"

Man, I'm chattering like a monkey!

"Yeah." She pulls up the right leg of her jeans. A bleeding sidewalk burn.

"Ouch."

"Yeah. It stings."

Her Texas accent makes two syllables out of one and she manages a slanting smile.

"Here, I've got some antiseptic ointment in my backpack."

Yes, I'm the nerdiest of all nerds.

"It's not one of those burning kinds is it?"

"Nope."

She leans back in relief. "Thanks."

"My name is Scotty, by the way."

"I'm Grace. Do you go to Marshall High?"

I hand her the tube of ointment. "Nah. I'm here with the film shoot."

"Wow. Really?"

"Uh-huh." I tell her about Charley, the TrailMama, road-school — my basic, ridiculous life — as she pats on the ointment. "I don't have a bandage."

I'm not that much of a nerd.

"It's okay. I'm headed inside anyway."

You know, every once in a while, you're pulled from your current reality by the realization you're experiencing something new and improved. Like now. I'm sitting here on a cement stoop in a small Texas town having a real-life conversation with a girl my age. A girl that attends a real-life high school.

"How old are you, Grace?"

"Sixteen."

"Me too!"

"Cool."

So she's not as excited about that fact as I am, and why would she be?

"So I hope you feel better. You live here?"

She jumps up. "No! I was just peeking in to have a look. They've been trying to rent the place out for months. It's empty."

"Oh." I thought she was headed inside? Maybe she just misspoke.

Maybe teenagers have a habit of looking into deserted houses clearly marked No Trespassing. I mean, what do I know? I want to ask her a thousand questions, but my tongue sits like an anvil in my mouth, and despite my deep desire, I cannot.

I stand up too. "Well, I'd better get down to the museum. I'm doing research for history."

"Good luck on that. Sounds cool."

"Thanks. Maybe I'll see you around."

"Maybe, but I live on the other side of town. So see ya."

"Okay."

Once down the steps, I hop on my scooter and finish descending the hill. Hotel Ginocchio, here I come.

Securing my scooter to a nearby light pole, and thank goodness for light poles, I look up the street. Grace is gone.

Thirty minutes later . . .

I only half listen as the tour guide shares details about the hotel's history with me, and I know I'll have to come back soon and hear it all over again. But I do take note of the fact that the manager, seated in his office on the second floor, had a clear shot down to the safe behind the desk on the first.

Were things different back then or what?

Well, maybe not. I mean my own father was shot down in cold blood. And it probably didn't go so much differently for Babette, my mother. Poor Charley, putting such a brave face on things all these years.

But still. I mean, nobody saw Babette get shot, right? Maybe she was kidnapped by the mob and she escaped before they could kill her. It's a possibility, right?

You're just grasping at straws, Scotty.

Whatever that stupid phrase means. What straws? What could they possibly be talking about?

I can't keep my mind on my schoolwork. The tour guide, a perfectly nice man who looks like he stepped out of the Civil War, has turned into the teacher from *Charlie Brown*. I mean, really, would one more day hurt? Doesn't reading F. Scott Fitzgerald count?

I would say yes.

I've got to get my mind off things, just sink into a great novel and forget about the drama going on right in my own life. And God, if you're up there, would you please not let the Karissa ruin this shoot? Can I maybe never cross paths with her? Can you make it really easy for me?

Okay, I went over the line with that last request. God never makes it easy on people. Even I know that.

What better place to read than a coffee shop? I follow Dee's directions and sail up to Jacob and Luke's Coffee. It's the cutest place, a squat, white Victorian home (and yeah, this town is totally back in time, the 1800s that is) with a circular porch to the right of the green front door.

I'm sweating like crazy and I know my Irish skin is going to burn like crazy when I take my shower tonight.

"Excuse me," an elderly lady says, smiling as she exits.

I step to the side as a parade of women follow, the same novel tucked under a few arms, and wouldn't it be fun to be a part of a book club? We're never in the same place long enough for those kinds of activities.

I used to feel lonely. I still do. But I'm sad now that I know how much of my real life I've missed out on. And maybe a little angry, too. And I can try to put the happy face on, but let's face it, I deserve to feel this way.

Inside, shades of gold and green and even turquoise, corrugated tin, and scratchy old wood decorate the large, funky room. I order a whole-milk latte and try to decide which "smash"—panini sandwich—to order. Yeah, very cute. The spirit of Charley whispers, "Order the veggie smash, order the veggie smash." I flick her out of the way like an annoying fly.

"I'll take Jacob's Reuben Smash."

The man behind the counter nods and punches a button on the cash register. "It's my favorite. But I made one slight change from the traditional Reuben."

I lean forward and whisper, "Are you Jacob then?"

He nods, winks. "But don't let on."

We laugh out loud.

"So what's the change?"

"You tell me after you've taken a bite."

"Deal."

He hands me my receipt. "Jeanne will bring it to the table when it's ready."

Jeanne sets down my latte. She's beautiful, an almost dead ringer for Kristin Scott Thomas. Short, sandy-blonde hair and one of those assured attitudes every woman hopes they have. At least I imagine they do. I sure do, anyway. Smiley eyes. Really pretty and a prime example of why Hollywood women are so wrong to go so plastic—her laugh lines make me want to laugh too. "Here you go, sweetie. Sandwich will be right up."

I head up the steps to the left of the coffee bar and into what must have once been a sun porch. Windows line the room and I choose one of two totally vintage, totally cool, green Naugahyde chairs, each back bull's-eyed with a three-inch wide, fabulous button. You just gotta love those crazy fifties designers, don't you? I set my latte on the rattan ottoman, pull out *Tender Is the Night*, and steep myself in the languor of summer on the French Riviera.

It couldn't have been any hotter there than it is here.

I hear a commotion down on the main floor. And I am so pulled out of warm sands and rich people, some certifiably crazy, others just silly, lying around in the sun, leaving me to wonder why on earth they deserved all that money in the first place!

Jeanne's head appears in the stairwell, then her neck, chest, waist and finally the rest of her as she climbs the steps. "Here we go. Jacob's Famous Reuben."

"So what's the difference?"

She sets the sandwich on the ottoman. "I'll give you a hint. It's about the cheese."

"Oh, I'm all about the cheese!"

"Then you'll guess it right away." She crosses her arms. "Go ahead. Take a bite."

I do, crunching through the fresh smashed and grilled rye bread, my teeth slicing through Russian dressing, sauerkraut, cheese, and layers of moist corned beef and oh, my goodness, does Charley really know what she's missing?

I start to really taste the ingredients, closing my eyes to segment the tastes, particularly the cheese. Oh, yes. It's clear, so very clear.

I open my eyes. "Got it."

"Well?"

"He used Provolone."

She smacks one hand down onto the leg of her blue jeans. "Yes! That's it. Good job." She cocks her head toward the stairwell and the increasing commotion.

"What's going on down there?"

"I think it's a famous actress. From the film shoot. You heard about the film shoot?"

I explain.

"Oh." She crosses her arms. "Well, then maybe you can tell me who this gal is. Acts like she's running the world in that Paris Hilton sort of way."

"Blonde and skinny?" Which describes seventy-five percent of Hollywood.

"But with a big chest that doesn't match the rest of her."

"Yes. That's Karissa Bonano."

She must have had more plastic surgery on her chest while she was in "rehab." And for the life of me, if someone would rather claim she's in rehab than getting plastic surgery, that just goes to show how screwed up things have become!

Jeanne throws her weight on one leg. "I must be out of touch. I've never heard of her."

"She's been around forever."

"How old is she?"

"Nineteen."

Jeanne throws out a full-on laugh. "Nineteen? She could be my child. Believe me, that is *not* forever ago! You know her?"

"Yeah. Kinda."

"Want me to tell her you're up here?"

"No way. Please, please, please don't do that!"

"I don't blame you. Mum's the word."

A few minutes later, the Karissa materializes in much the same manner Jeanne did. I raise my book to hide my face.

She's by herself. Nobody follows.

Well, this is Marshall, Texas. I doubt people get excited about a Hollywood teen queen beyond the shock of first sight. At least that's what I think, anyway. They seem way too normal.

Her phone rings and I prepare myself to shamelessly eavesdrop, which means I poke my nose even farther into the pages of my book.

"Hey, Linds."

Lindsay Lohan? Maybe.

"No, I'm here already. This town is about as exciting as Early American furniture."

Okay, I didn't think her capable of that kind of simile.

"What are you up to?"

As if anybody would *really* want to know.

"You saw him? On the lot? How'd he look?"

Who's he?

"They cut his curls off for the role? That's terrible. How does it look?"

What curls?

I turn my back on Karissa and grab my laptop off the ottoman. Googling *Seth Haas*, I find the latest picture of him, head shorn close. No! No way! She cannot possibly still be interested in him.

And yes, he's still cute.

"So what did he say?"

That he never wants to see you again, you lying wench, after catching you with cocaine at the last shoot. What do you expect him to say?

"Well, that's encouraging. Sort of, you know?"

It better not be. I'm so texting Seth as soon as I get away from the Karissa and her phone friend, whoever it may be. It's probably not Lindsay Lohan at all. It's probably her cousin Lindsay from Springfield, Illinois, or something.

"I gotta go. I've got lines to learn for tomorrow and I found a quiet spot in a coffee shop. . . Just some bookworm here in the room with me." She whispers that last line.

Well, I've got to hand it to her, at least she knows a book when she sees one.

I'm just sayin'.

I sneak a peek at her.

"What?" she says, then examines her fingernails as she listens to "Linds." "Oh, I haven't figured out what my issue is going to be yet. Nothing too controversial though. Maybe something to do with animals. Everybody loves animals."

On my way out, Karissa still tucked up in one of the blue chairs in the corner (and boy was I careful to keep my back turned to her when I packed up), Jacob hails me from the counter. "Come here!"

"Sure."

"I packed you up some dinner. Jeanne told me about you living in an RV and all that, and your mom bein' all busy right now."

"You didn't have to do that."

"It's no big deal. I had some chicken salad ready to go to waste if I didn't serve it up today."

"Thanks. I love chicken salad. I love mayo." I smell inside the brown paper bag. "I smell some red pepper in there."

"Bingo. Marinated red pepper on that sandwich. Jeanne told me you guessed the cheese."

I take stock of Jacob. I guess he's in his midforties, light brown hair with a smattering of silver by the ears. Lots of hair. Long eyelashes, a thin, kind face. "Why are you being so nice?"

"I don't know. You just have that look about you."

"What look?"

"A vagabond sadness."

Well, why don't you just come out and say it, Jacob? Nice word choice, by the way.

He pats the counter. "Jeanne says you're homeschooled."

"Sort of. I do most of the work myself."

"Having any trouble in anything? I homeschooled my own son for years. Right here in the store."

"Math has always been the bane of my existence, and I need a music credit too."

"Music?" He rests his forearms on the counter's edge.

"I play no instrument whatsoever. Don't read music. And have no real appreciation for it. Classical music, that is."

"Meet me here at the shop tomorrow at closing time. You want music appreciation, I'll give you music appreciation."

"Really? Okay! I'll be here."

I check the sign on the way out. Six p.m.

I turn back around. "Who's your favorite musical artist of all time?"

"Can only be one answer to that question. Elvis Presley."

Oh yes, this is good. This is very, very good.

"'Love me tender, love me sweet . . .'" he sings.

"'Never let me go.'" I finish the line.

Babette loved Elvis. Charley says she used to sing me to sleep with this very song.

You have made my life complete.

And I love you so.

———————

After wandering around town for the rest of the afternoon, reading by the courthouse and getting another coffee at Weisman's, it's time to get back. I jump off the scooter, bound up into the TrailMama, and change into something a little special. Grampie is picking me up in ten minutes. Didn't plan on getting hung up at the thrift store on Washington Street. *Dan Cohen's Bare Necessities Hi-Style Fashions.* It isn't really called that. But it seems that once a business settles in that space, it never completely vacates. Dan Cohen's Shoes still presents itself via white block tile letters on the pavement by the entrance. Hi-Style Fashions glimmers in gold capital letters on slate above the plate-glass window, but the window itself tells the real tale. In point of fact, I wandered about the racks at Bare Necessities.

So you know I love vintage. And while the pickings were slimmer than Victoria Beckham's thighs, a yellow and green paisley belt, stamped leather and so very eighties in a good way, and a pair of yellow fifties kitten-heel pumps begged me to rescue them from the riff-raff of intarsia sweaters and pinstriped, peg-legged jeans. Some fashions, no matter how popular in their original manifestations, deserve no encore performance.

But now I'm running behind. I dig through my Rubbermaid tub for a pair of grey trousers, 1940s, and my gold cardigan sweater, 1960. Accompanied by the new belt and pumps and a French twist in my hair?

I'm just sayin'!

Now that I'm sixteen, Charley says it's okay to wear a little makeup. Hey, I told you she was all about the natural. I'm not comfortable with it yet, so a little blush and some lip gloss will work. Really, with these thick glasses, all the eyeliner in the world wouldn't matter. Maybe if we harkened back to those raccoon eyes that were popular a couple of years ago it would make a difference, but with my reading until two in the morning night after night, I need no help with dark circles.

Oh yeah, some cover-up. I'm using cover-up now too.

Charley practically falls across the threshold. "Someone tell me the day's almost over!"

"The day's almost over."

"No. It isn't. Two more scenes to go and Whataburger's getting miffed because we're ordering fifty hamburgers at a time!"

I set down my blush and hop down from my bunk. "Let me pour you some limeade. I just made it this morning."

"From fresh limes?"

Okay, so she must not be that tired. "No."

"You know"—she sits at the dinette and rubs her eyes with the heels of her hands (no mascara on those lashes)—"I don't even care. Just pour me a long one, baby. No ice."

Lots of sugar. She'd freak if she knew how much. But she could sure use the pick-me-up.

I pull down a green plastic cup, dollar-store special, fill it almost to the rim and set it in front of her.

As the cool liquid slides down her throat, I can almost visibly see her freshening. Very nice.

"Mmm! That was really good!"

"Stick with me, Charley."

"We don't have much choice, do we, baby?"

The tension intrudes.

I climb back up to finish with the lip gloss. "You haven't heard more about Biker Guy, have you?"

"Nope. I think we lost him in Memphis." Color rises from her throat up to her forehead. "Oh, that's much better. What did you put in that drink?"

"A little bit of fresh lemon." Pah, pah. Lip gloss in place.

"Groovy. Gotta go."

I jump back down, reach into the fridge and hand her a soy yogurt. "Take this. You're getting too skinny and despite popular Hollywood opinion, you *can* be too skinny."

She gives me one of her wide grins. I love my grandmother, especially now that I know she's not my mother. She makes a lousy mother, but a really great grandmother.

"Where are you going tonight? I thought I told you to stay close to the RV."

"Grammie and Grampie are in town."

"Are you sure it's safe?"

"Oh, come on, Charley. We love them!"

"That's true. Okay, then, I guess it's okay. I've got to go." She kisses my cheek and rushes out the door.

Throwing my cardigan around my shoulders, I head down to the Paramount, Marshall's old-time, now-defunct movie theater, complete with light-bulbed marquis. Man, these shoes are already killing me.

But I'm sixteen. I'll learn to deal.

Grampie must have seen me in his side mirror, because he jumps out of the driver's side of the Tracker. And yes, I'm meeting them here because Charley insisted nobody should know exactly where we're camped. As if Grampie and Grammie couldn't find a movie setup in a town the size of Marshall. Of course, I didn't say *a word*.

"Scotty!"

I just run. Run, run right toward him, slamming myself into him after jumping over the drainage grate. He smells so good. Like his pipe tobacco and Dentyne cinnamon gum. Dove soap too. "Oh, Grampie. Grampie." I just breathe him in and feel his warm arms embrace me.

"Now, wait, wait! Group hug!" Grammie scoots around the vehicle and her arms encircle us both.

I love them.

I love them because they're the type of people who wait for me to release the embrace. They grill my favorite food. They have fluffy blankets and pillows in their RV. And I swear, we could stand here all night if I didn't move. I don't. I'm giving it another full minute.

You see, these dear old people love me.

This spring, Grammie took me shopping for an awful, aqua-blue chiffon formal, and I danced the night away at the RV park's activities center. Me and Grampie stole the show. They took me to Kitty Hawk and let me eat all the meat and cheese I wanted; they sequestered me from Biker Guy. Grampie misted up several times.

Grammie doesn't mist up much. She must get that out on her poetry and dime-store romances. But she feels deeply as you can see in the glowing centers of her fading brown eyes.

I pull back.

"Oh you guys! You're here!" My smile practically divides my face in two. "Grammie, you look great!"

She's worn a turban ever since I've known her, but now, her hair foams around her head in a curly, snowy almost-afro. "You like?" She pats her head.

"I love it. I didn't know you had all that curly hair! Why did you hide it for so long?"

She straightens her caftan, parrot green with gold and silver embroidery. "You inspired me this summer, letting all those curls of yours roam free! I said to George, 'I just should do that too.' And he said"—her voice deepens—"'I've been saying that for years, my darling.'"

I pull them into another hug. Grampie's navy blue sports coat, probably forty years old at least, lies soft under my cheek. And he looks so dapper with that cranberry silk cravat at his neck. Grampie, ahem, George Roberts Wethington, made his own way in the world, surely. But he's from old stock, as they say. Just stubborn enough to want to prove he could do it himself. And he did. He invented all sorts of things for machines we probably use every day. Now he writes travel articles for AARP and other magazines. Hence their life on the road. He uses library computers to type up and send in his work. For someone so hip, he's technologically hopeless.

"Where are we going tonight?"

"How about back to the Hitchin' Post?" Grampie.

"The *Hitchin'* Post?"

Grammie squeezes my shoulder. "It's the RV park. A sweet little place. And George is marinating steaks for the grill."

"Let's go!"

Dear Elaine,

Everything's quiet on the lot. Most of the cast and crew are staying at the Best Western Executive. Except for Karissa, who insisted Jeremy rent an entire B&B for her. She's hogging it up at the Three Oaks Bed and Breakfast, all by her lonesome. Even Cillian Murphy's at the Best Western. I haven't met him yet, but Charley says he's really nice.

Oh, I had the best time with Grammie and Grampie, until . . . Well, I've got to admit that something's just up with them. I decided to tell them all about Babette and my father and what went down, how he was shot by the mob in front of some gubernatorial candidate who's running for president now, and since we're only gearing up for the primaries the guy could be one of about ten men. Anyway, Elaine, Grammie started to cry and had to leave the room. Grampie followed her and left me sitting there with my steak, wondering why the upset. He came out a few minutes later, eyes all red-rimmed, sympathy tears, I guess, and apologized. Told me Grammie had a close relative murdered a long time ago, and it all just sort of took her by surprise. We ate our dessert in front of the satellite TV and Grampie brought me home on his own. I hope I haven't offended them. Because, Elaine, I hate to admit it, but I need Grammie and Grampie. They're my family. I don't know if they realize it.

Maybe Babette would understand. I'd probably just have walked into the camper and told her all about it.

Hollywood Nobody: Wednesday, September 17

And oh, do you even wanna know, Nobodies? Of course you do!

Karissa Bonano has landed in a small Texas town and Little Me ain't tellin' which one! Yesterday she was seen at the hippest coffee shop there, nose in a script and ear to a cell phone, talking subterfuge to Lindsay Lohan about none other than her two-beaus-ago lovelight, Seth *Hottie* Haas. The Karissa seems to think she has a prayer with the most gorgeous guy in Hollywood right now. What do you think?

The Nasty Baldwin Brother decided to take his own cell phone privileges away. Okay, that's not true. Would that it were. Here he is walking alone on Hollywood Boulevard. Need I say more?

A mass memorial service at Hollywood Forever Cemetery is

set tomorrow honoring those stars who passed away but who still influence the industry today. On its face this seems very nice. But Little Me has to wonder, where does it end? Aren't there enough award shows already? Is this another ploy in the big publicity machine to bring a little class back to Tinseltown because, as we know, only a handful of actors have it these days, and the only place to find it is the cemetery? I'm just sayin'.

Today's Rant: George Clooney, Leonardo DiCaprio, Jessica Simpson, and Britney Spears. I don't care which side of the aisle they're on, I'm tired of hearing celebrity opinions on politics. Because here's the deal: with a few exceptions, the opinions are coming out of the mouths of people who are thought to have absolutely no ability to function without drugs, plastic surgery, conspicuous consumerism, and an addiction to acclaim. They'd do better for their pet issues by simply keeping their mouths shut. Even when I agree with them they get on my nerves.

Today's Violette Dillinger Report: It's confirmed. Violette's dating Joe Mason, lead singer and guitarist for mild punk band Nice Margaret. Let's hope this new couple lasts longer than Ms. Reid and whoever it is she's dating this afternoon.

Today's Quote: "It's good to experience Hollywood in short bursts, I guess. Little snippets. I don't think I can handle being here all the time. It's pretty nutty." Johnny Depp

Busy day for me, Nobodies! I'll check in with you soon! Later!

Wednesday, September 17

Was yesterday crazy or what? I met tons of new people. So many, in fact, my head was reeling when I woke up. Huge meat headache. So I took some ibuprofen and climbed back in bed until two when my phone went off. Text message.

Seth: Where r u?

Me: In bed.

Seth: Sick?

Me: Under the weather.

Seth: Srry. gues wht. i'll b thr in 3 dys.

What? Oh my gosh! Keep cool, Scotty.

Me: That's great. Are you flying in?

Seth: Dallas. will rnt a car.

Me: Cool. Text me as soon as you land!

Seth: Will do.

Me: See ya!

Seth: C ya!

And no mention of the Karissa! I throw down the phone and get going on school, right there in the TrailMama, boning up on music appreciation, because in four hours, Jacob and I are meeting for lessons.

———

I'm sitting in my funky chair at Jacob and Luke's, feet up on the ottoman, reading *Tender Is the Night*, and oh, my gosh, that Nicole woman sure knew how to hide her craziness. I was shocked when I got to the middle of the book and there she is, certifiably nuts.

What is it with adults and secrets all the time, huh? I've grown up inside a secret so large, I can sort of understand. But that secret wasn't/isn't really my secret. I'm just embroiled unwittingly in the whole affair.

Embroiled unwittingly. I like it.

And what a user the woman is. Poor Dick Diver. You know, Fitzgerald had some crazy women populating his books. They're users, every last one of them I've read about so far. I should be used to that by now with Hollywood.

But I'm not. And hopefully I never will be.

"Hey, Scotty! You ready?" Jacob stops at the top of the steps.

"Absolutely."

Jeanne's letting herself out of the shop as we descend the stairs.

"Good night, Jeanne! See you tomorrow." Jacob.

"'Night y'all."

She shuts the screen door.

"I thought she was your wife."

"Jeanne? No, she's married to a biology professor. We go way back, though. Graduates of Marshall High, 1975."

"Oh. Are you married, then?"

"I was. Got divorced years ago."

"So you must have had custody if you homeschooled your son."

"Can't pull anything over on you, I'm guessing."

"Never."

I follow him into the kitchen. "Where's your son now?"

"Luke started college this fall."

"Luke? That explains the shop name. So why did your wife give up custody?"

He opens the fridge and pulls out a block of cheese and some ham. "She didn't. She was killed on the way home from work the day after the divorce was finalized."

I honestly want to giggle. I don't know why. I mean, it's so tragic, but so . . . I don't know, so movie-plot-like. Still, I'm as good an actor as the Karissa.

"So you're a widower."

"Technically, no. I'm a divorcee."

"But just one day."

"Nope. Can't accept that."

"Okay."

He takes out a loaf of rye bread and begins cutting off slices. "You're even more curious than I thought."

"Just can't seem to let go." I shrug.

"Good for you. You keep that quality with you, Scotty, and you'll do all right."

"Thanks."

I feel warm and squidgy inside.

Thirty minutes later . . .

Sandwiches eaten and dishes done, Jacob grabs a stack of CDs from the coffee shop's stereo cabinet below the counter.

"Okay, I was kidding about Elvis." Jacob hands me the CDs as I sit down on a parson's bench beneath a pink chandelier. I spread them out on the table.

Bach. Mozart. Beethoven. Schumann. Copeland. Vaughan

Williams. Stravinsky. Wagner.

I tap the Wagner CD. "Wasn't he crazy?"

"As a loon!"

More crazy people.

"Let's start with Beethoven," I say.

"You got it."

He slides the jewel case off the table and disappears behind the counter.

I glance at the piano on which a sign says, Play Only If You Can. "Jacob, do you play an instrument?"

"Piano," he says, his head popping back up into view.

"Will you play for me?"

"What about Beethoven?"

"He can go second."

Jacob smiles and swings his lean body back around the counter. He plops down on the bench. "Any requests?"

"Something Elvis."

His hands, graceful and long-fingered, move across the keys and the melody to "Love Me Tender" fills the room.

Then he sings.

Jacob's voice, soft and expressive, tells the story of the first four verses, but right before the last he glances at me and grins.

"When at last your dreams come true, Scotty, this I know, happiness will follow you, everywhere you go."

He finishes with a piano flourish, and even though he did the corny Scotty name change, which totally warrants a hug, I give him the standing ovation instead.

"Aw, thanks, Scotty." Is that the cutest, shyest smile in the world, or what? Someone should snatch this guy up. I can't imagine what these East Texas women are thinking.

Jacob returns to the stereo, and a few seconds later, some of the most haunting strains of music I've ever heard fill the room.

"What is it?"

"*Moonlight Sonata.*"

"It's beautiful."

"Just listen, Scotty. Sit back. Close your eyes and let it wash over you."

I do just that.

The notes tug at my sad heart, the sadness enveloping my needy soul, and I appreciate what it's doing. I rest in its beauty, pictures of who I imagine Babette to be and my father. I see us walking hand in hand through an early evening forest, sunlight strewn in ribbons through the leaves and onto the forest floor. They swing me and say, "That-a-girl."

I open my eyes after the last notes of the first movement fade. "I need to go home now."

Jacob walks me out to my scooter. "Are you okay, Scotty?"

"I've never had music affect me that way before."

"It does that to you sometime." He points to my backpack, in which I've placed the other CDs. "A little Schumann will cure up the melancholy if you need it to."

"No. No, thanks, Jacob. I'm thinking this feels right, right about now."

Midnight . . .

Lucky for me the TrailMama came equipped with a stereo system. A Bach fugue, don't ask me which one, I lost track of the tracks, bounces off the fiberglass walls.

Charley enters; her eyes widen. "Classical music?" I jump up from the lounge chair and flip off the music.

"Thought I'd expand my musical horizon."

"Groovy, baby."

"Well, it's really not groovy, per se . . ."

"You know what I mean." She sets down her knapsack and reaches into the refrigerator, where a fresh pitcher of my special limeade awaits. "Oh good!"

"Why don't you take a shower and I'll pour you a glass."

"Thanks."

There's a reason for my niceness. I want to find out more about my family. Charley's always been tight-lipped about my father, but I thought it was because I was illegitimate or something, or she was a widow and it was all too painful. Okay, the second thought was implausible. What widow wouldn't tell her child who her father was? But, missing my father as I've always done, who could blame me for trying to think up any reason, good or not, for her silence?

I pour the drink, slice a couple of rounds off a lemon and drown them in the liquid.

She comes back dressed in a long T-shirt, her hair up in a towel. "That was just what I needed. I can't tell you how tired I am." She picks up the glass, raises it before her eyes and squints. "Lemon slices? Okay, baby, what do you want? Are you going to try and convince me to let you eat cheese again? Because if you are, I've got to lay it down straight. I'm still not on board with the idea."

"No. It's not about cheese, Charley."

Especially having eaten three extra slices after my sandwich.

We sit at the dinette.

She takes a long sip. "Oh, that's so good. Okay, so what is it?"

"I want to find out more about my father."

"Baby, I've told you everything I know."

"Not about his parents. I have a whole other set of grandparents, don't I?"

She shrugs. "I don't know."

"What? How could you not know this?"

"He lived a very secret life, Scotty. Your father and Babette eloped after dating only three weeks."

"Really? That's so romantic!"

She smiled. "I thought so too. She was scared to tell me."

"No way! It sounds like something *you* would do!"

"It's true."

"But how did you not know my father's parents?"

Tears well up in her eyes. "Scotty, I'm not sure if you can understand this. But Babbie, your mom, well, she had a whole other life apart from me. I embarrassed her, I think. She never said that, but . . . baby, I'm just a flighty old hippie. Back in those days, I . . ." She searches the ceiling for what to say next. "Baby, . . ." She breathes deep. "I went from man to man. I . . . tried to . . . I'm so sorry."

Oh, man. "Charley, you really don't have to go on."

"No. You've got to know she did the right thing. Babbie . . . well, she wanted to protect you, she really did. And she didn't want to embarrass your dad or herself. I never met your other grandparents, baby. I didn't go to Christmas at your house; you all didn't come to Thanksgiving at mine. Babbie would meet me with you at the park or at the Inner Harbor and we'd have lunch.

She'd let me push you on the swings." She tries to smile her sweet smile. "I lived for Thursdays. I'd wear the most normal clothing I could find and we'd have the best times. But always at the end of the day she'd ask me if Ray was still living with me, or Gary or whoever it was at the time. Finally, one day I said, 'He's gone. They're all gone. I want you and Ariana in my life, Babbie. Really in my life.'"

"So then there were the Thanksgivings and Christmases after that, right?"

She shakes her head. "That was two weeks before the shooting. It was the first night she'd ever left you with me. I was so happy about the decision I'd made to kick Gary out. He was bad news. They all were, baby."

I don't know what to say.

"I'm sorry, Scotty."

"Did my mother know who her father was?"

"No. I didn't either." She reaches for my hand and I reach out for hers. "She never really forgave me for that. And I was doomed to repeat the same mistake for you. I mean, you thought I didn't know."

"But it wasn't your fault with me."

"No. But it had the same effect, didn't it?"

"Yeah. I guess it did."

It's so still here in the camper. The world has shut down inside and out. "Charley, can I sleep with you tonight?"

"Sure, baby."

"Let's go to bed."

I follow her into her little bedroom and climb into her bed first like when I was tiny. I snuggle into her, just like I used to as well.

Life is what it is. People make mistakes, but most times, it just seems like the heartache lasts forever.

Hollywood Nobody: Thursday, September 18

Today's News: It was a huge day in Hollywood yesterday. One of Hollywood's hottest couples filed for divorce. Who? A free copy of <u>Violette Dillinger's</u> CD to the first person who leaves the answer in the comments. Speaking of Violette, she told me, "I may just be in love with Joe." Let's hope this romance lasts longer than unpasteurized milk. We're with you, Violette!

<u>Jeremy Winger</u>'s set is buzzing with activity. The Karissa has arrived and is already causing a stir in the costume department because of a change in her bust measurements. Catering is ready to quit because nothing suits Miss Queen's fancy. Get a <u>Whataburger</u> is all I can say, Karissa. Little Me is steering clear of the Teen Nightmare as much as possible. Some accidents we don't want to slow down to watch.

Oh, and despite the fact that the Karissa fouled up any chance she had with Seth Haas at last spring's shoot for *Green Light*, the upcoming remake of *The Great Gatsby*, she's got high hopes she can rope him in here in the wilds of Texas. Maybe the heat will get her first. Here's hoping.

Today's Rant: This is a serious rant, Nobodies. Another runway model died of heart failure yesterday in Brazil. At 5′ 11″, <u>Christiana Ramirez</u> weighed 98 pounds. Despite the intervention of her parents, she wasn't able to kick her eating disorder. She was only twenty years old. So I don't want to hear all these emaciated celebrities who were once normal-looking people drone on about the fact that they don't diet, that they're at their normal weight, that they have high metabolisms. Bull! Stop the solidarity crap and tell us the truth. Do you honestly think we're sitting here watching you, believing a word you say? You know what they call people who continue to lie even when everyone around them knows they're lying? Sociopaths. You're setting an example whether you want to or not. And one more thing, stop insulting our intelligence. We've had quite enough of that.

Today's Quote: "I'm very glad I'm a normal-sized person, and I shall continue to be a normal-sized person, enjoying my food." Kate Winslet

Okay, I've given you this quote before. But the woman's a genius!

Later!

Thursday, September 18, 7:00 p.m.

I slide into the backseat of Grammie and Grampie's Tracker. "I'm ready!"

"Good!" Grammie turns around in her seat up front. "You look great! I see you're taking a lesson from me now!"

Yes, my hair is a cloud with one of Charley's head wraps holding back the front. "You got it. I thought we'd make a big hair entrance to the game. I mean, we *are* in Texas."

Grampie hoots.

"So what are we seeing and how in the world did you already find out about the local high school's sports schedule?"

Grampie puts the car in drive and pulls out onto Washington Street. "Hey, Grammie and I don't let any grass grow under our feet. Life's too short at our age."

Grammie looks at me. "At any age."

"That's the truth. So what are we watching? Football? Soccer? Basketball?"

"Honey, we're in Texas. Football all the way." Grammie.

Grampie clears his throat. "Scotty, honey, basketball is a winter sport."

"Oh, George, how would Scotty know that?"

And this is why I love Grammie so much.

I'm going to a high school football game. A real high school football game. I can hardly believe it.

Bright lights. A big green field. Glaring white lines. A band marching around, cheerleaders, pom-poms, shouts, and then the team will come running onto the field.

Several minutes later, having driven across town (and yeah, that's how small Marshall is) we pull into Marshall High's parking lot and follow a stream of people into the football stadium.

Red abounds here. Obviously the school color.

The mascot? The Mavericks.

Yeah, I could like it here.

Other than the stares our hair is getting. And I don't think this pink, tiered lace skirt with boots is a normal find down in these parts. Oh, well. At least I'm with Grammie and Grampie.

"Excuse me," somebody says from behind as we begin to

ascend into the bleachers.

I look over my shoulder. "Grace?"

Her brows rise. "Scotty, right?"

"Uh-huh."

"I was just trying to get by. My boyfriend's up there."

We step to the side. Grampie says, "Far be it from us to stand in the way of romance."

She runs up the steps, climbs over the top row's occupants and sits down next to . . . well, he's cute . . . but . . . okay, really good-looking . . . but . . . he reaches up, grabs her forearm and pulls her roughly down onto the seat beside him.

"There's a spot!" Grammie says a little too loudly. A sea of Texans look our way. But the sweetest couple in America charms them as we scoot between their bent knees and the backs of the people in front of them, eighty percent of them clothed in something red.

It's all just like I imagine. Just like *Remember the Titans* or *Friday Night Lights*.

The band plays the fight song, the team breaks through a paper banner two cheerleaders stretch across the opening to the field, and pom-poms flicker and bob to the beat of the music.

A woman walks up the steps and starts down the row in front of us, smiling and chatting to some of the students. Must be a teacher. Imagine the slim, yet tensile strength of a willow tree, its slender beauty and grace as the wind blows its branches, and you've got a good picture of who they're calling Miss Foster. Somebody asks her how the fall play is coming.

"Wonderfully. We have such talented students."

She's obviously a dancer, the way she moves her hands so fluidly. And her voice is lyrical, musical, and respectful. She's dressed in a tight-fitting black shirt with a boat neck, very Audrey Hepburn, black pedal pushers and black ballet flats. Her dark hair, pulled up at the front, cascades down her back, very Juliet.

I lean over toward Grammie. "She must be the drama teacher. Don't you just love her?"

"She's fabulous, dear!"

"I'll bet you were just as fabulous when you were her age."

Grampie says, "She was. And is."

Definitely.

Taking Grammie's hand, I lean sideways and rest my head against her arm. She puts her arm around me and holds me close as the color and life of a small-town community passes before us in its grand array.

It's one of the best nights of my life.

Hey, I've lived a very sheltered life!

The final whistle blows. The Mavericks won! Soon enough, the crowd begins to file out. "Can we just stay and watch awhile?" I ask. "I'd like to see the lights go out."

"Of course, dear." Grammie.

Grace and her boyfriend walk down the steps without a glance in our direction. Not that I'd expect anything different.

But still.

On the last step, he pushes her and she shoots forward off the step, catching herself just before she goes down completely.

"Cody!" she yells.

He throws back his head, points at her, and laughs.

"Did you see that?" I ask Grammie and Grampie.

"Shameful." Grampie.
"What a pig." Grammie.
Yeah. What a pig.

Hollywood Nobody: Friday, September 19

Congratulations to Hollywood Junkie, who won <u>Violette Dillinger's</u> album yesterday!

So, Nobodies, not much to report today, other than <u>Pamela Anderson</u> and Tommy Lee were seen with their kids and everyone's wondering if they'll finally get back together. I've got to be honest, even Pam was too classy for <u>Kid Rock</u>. Was anybody surprised when that one broke up?

Violette Dillinger will be appearing tonight on <u>Jay Leno</u>. Make sure to tune in. What will her T-shirt say? She's getting known for them nowadays. My favorite: Saying People Suck Is Mean. Gotta love that one.

Today's News: A <u>baby</u> was left in one of the hallways of Cedars-Sinai Hospital yesterday in LA. Nobody is coming forward to claim the little girl doctors say is around three months old. With the stars and the new fad of humanitarianism, is anybody wondering whether someone in need of publicity right now will claim her? Cynical? Uh, ya think?

Today's Rant: <u>Barbie</u> dolls. I was online yesterday thinking about Barbie dolls. Does anybody else think they look like "ladies of the evening"? And why do parents want their daughters to pretend with the likes of Barbie? Those measurements? That hair? Please. It makes us feel inferior from age five!

Today's Quote: "In Hollywood, the women are all peaches. It makes one long for an apple occasionally." W. Somerset Maugham

<u>Seth Hottie Haas</u> was seen with comedian Bill Blanch last night at The Viper Room. According to my sources they looked like boys on the prowl. The Karissa ain't going to like that one bit. Sorry, Miss K, but apparently Seth has other plans.

Today's Kudo: Betty White. She's as old as my grandmother's baby shoes, but don't you just love her on those pet store commercials? Betty, will you be my great-grandmother?

Later!

Friday, September 19

Now, I'm betting that the Karissa reads my blog. My subscriptions have soared and some of the other blogs are starting to list me in their links. Michael from B-Listers e-mails me sometimes and said he doesn't mind if I share his pictures as long as I give him credit. Pretty cool.

Charley sets a plate of whole-wheat pancakes in front of me. "I'm sorry I've been so busy. Have you been starving?"

"Hardly!" I reach for the sliced strawberries. Too much sugar in maple syrup for Charley's liking.

After spooning the fruit on top of the stack, I cut out a wedge. Hmm. About the driest breakfast ever. Other than fifty-six grain toast with nothing on it. But she means well.

Charley falls into the meal like Rachael Ray made it or something. Well, at least somebody's enjoying it for real. I'm pretending my head off.

"So how's the shoot going?"

"I've got the day off. Well, sort of. I don't have to be on set, but I've got to prepare for tomorrow."

"Jeremy loves having food in his films."

"Tell me about it." She reaches for the soymilk carton and pours us both glasses.

Okay, yes, I like soymilk. At least there's that.

"So how much of Karissa has disappeared by this time?"

"Oh, she's up to her elbows, but somehow still managing to eat the food, which is slowly going bad. By the end of the film" — she shudders — "it'll look like garbage."

"That sounds like fun. What's she been like?"

"Uppity. Even more so than at the last shoot. Without drugs she's meaner than before."

"Somehow that's not the right kind of role-model lesson."

She forks up another bite of pancakes. "If I thought for a minute you saw girls like Karissa as role models, we'd be doing something else."

"Really, Charley?"

"I'm more of a grown-up than I seem sometimes, baby."

She loves me. She really loves me.

"I think I'll go on set today." I cut another wedge of pancake.

"That would be cool. And you were right about Cillian Murphy. He's really nice. Cute too. In that pretty-boy way."

"Most definitely."

"Have you heard from Joy Overstreet?" she asks.

So that was random.

Background here: Joy and Jeremy had a thing going back at the last shoot, and it was all my fault. I got her a job as a seamstress to help Ms. Burrell. Jeremy took one look at her and that was that. Poor Charley, who has loved Jeremy forever.

"I got an e-mail the other day. She's back in New York. Found a financial backer for her line of plus-sized couture. And is still seeing Jeremy."

"Oh, that's so good! Good for her! And Jeremy really likes her a lot."

Honestly, I feel like I'm talking to a junior-high-school girl with just enough maturity to make it look like she's happy for all parties concerned.

My heart breaks for her. "Charley?"

"Yes, baby?"

"We're done pretending, okay? Can we stop pretending on all levels? Not just Biker Guy and Babette and my dad?"

Tears collect in her eyes. "Sure, Scotty."

"I know you love Jeremy. I know those other men were cheap substitutes. Weren't they?" *Please tell me yes. Please don't tell me you had so little respect for yourself anybody could walk all over you just because you just couldn't say no.* She nods.

"So why don't you tell him?"

"Well, he's fallen for Joy now—"

I lean back in my chair and cross my arms. "Well, I personally think he just doesn't pursue you because he thinks you don't want that."

"I don't. Not with all that we're running from."

"Then you're in a pickle, I guess."

She takes my hand and squeezes it. "You've nailed it, baby."

———————————

Before I head to the set, I zip on over to Jacob and Luke's for a cup of coffee and to go over my research notes on Beethoven. At ten thirty, it's not surprising the morning rush has cleared out. An older man sits at a table near the piano, his pen delicately licking a crossword puzzle. A few others sip their coffee before their open laptops, working on whatever it is people work on in coffee shops. Writers? Entrepreneurs? Students, surely, from over at East Texas Baptist University. And in the room off to the right, a few ladies sit with open Bibles and big workbooks. They're laughing together. I remind myself I've got to get out that Bible Grammie gave me. I lost track of things in Nashville. Was halfway through the book of Mark and didn't pick it back up again.

You know, Movie Jesus is a whole lot different from Bible Jesus.

I'm just sayin'.

Jeanne greets me from the counter. She wears cargo khakis, a dusky purple T-shirt, and a pair of funky silver earrings. "Scotty! You survived Elvis night, I see."

"I did." I approach the counter. "Actually, Jacob knows a lot about classical music."

"I thought maybe Jacob was giving you a virtual tour of Graceland."

"I love Graceland."

"You know, I don't know any other kid your age who loves Graceland. What'll you have today?"

"Soy caramel latte."

"Nice choice."

"Where's Jacob?"

"In the back making up the chicken salad." She glances at the front door. "Oh, good. Here she comes."

I turn my neck. "It's the drama teacher!"

"Wow, you get around quick."

"I went to the football game last night at Marshall High."

"Like I said."

"So she *is* the drama teacher? I was just guessing."

"Yeah." She leans forward. "Jacob has the biggest crush imaginable on that woman."

"Can you blame him?"

"No. But that's not the point. She's got the biggest crush on him too, but neither one knows about the other's feelings."

"No!"

"Yes!"

"What's her name?"

"Miss Foster."

I look back around. Miss Foster chats with the man doing the crossword puzzle. This morning she's wearing a pencil-thin black skirt and a white twin set. Her dark hair is pulled back into a butter-yellow scarf.

"Why don't you tell them?"

She leans back and looks at me as if I'm the most stupid person in the room, which I just may well be. But still. "Because it's more fun this way! Look at her! She's almost perfect but can't possibly see why Jacob would be interested in her. And Jacob. Well, you've been with him. He's the nicest guy ever and not bad looking to boot. He'll be turning fifty next year and I think he's lost his confidence." She straightens up as Miss Foster approaches. "Good morning, Phoebe! Your usual?"

Phoebe. And isn't that just perfect? I'm so loving this!

"Just tea today, Jeanne, and thanks."

"It'll be right up." Jeanne begins to make my drink. "How's play practice going?"

"Beautifully. Those kids are great."

"You sound way too enthusiastic." Jeanne.

Phoebe rolls her eyes.

I see inside them, I see the questions abounding. Why is someone of my talent in Marshall, at a high school? Why am I not taking a chance, going to New York or Hollywood? Is that level of the theater only for the brave? Am I not brave?

Then her eyes soften.

Jacob stands at the kitchen doorway, hands deep in his jeans pockets.

Ah. So that's why she stays here in this East Texas town.

Jacob's eyes glow with the same softness.

And this is why he hasn't remarried.

It's all so clear. So delightful and honest. Stuff like this doesn't happen in Hollywood, I bet. In Hollywood, you want something, you go for it, don't dare wait for the other party to make the first move.

The moment diffuses into the hard cold reality of caffeine ingestion as Jeanne slams the filter into place on the espresso machine.

I turn to Miss Foster. "I was at the football game last night."

"Wonderful! Do you go to MHS?" She lays a graceful hand on my shoulder. "I don't think I've seen you there."

"Nah. I'm here with the film crew."

Her face ignites with an equal mixture of surprise and delight.

"Film crew?"

Jeanne barks a laugh. "Where have you been, missy? They've been set up over on Wellington for almost a week."

I explain the situation a bit, like I've been doing nonstop since I've arrived.

"Is the director anybody I've heard of?"

"Jeremy Winger."

"No!" She gasps, placing her fingertips up to her mouth. "I love his work."

"He's a good guy."

"You know him?"

"He's been almost like a father to me."

Jacob walks up. "Hey, Scotty! Want me to look over your notes?"

"Sure."

"Wait!" Phoebe lays a hand on my arm. "I'd love to pick your brain. Can I buy your coffee and we can talk?"

"Most definitely. I'd be an idiot to turn down an offer like that."

Jeanne hands me my drink. "I'll say!"

Jacob says, "Hi, Phoebe. The Mavericks won again, huh?"

"Of course they did! Jacob you look so nice today. I love that yellow shirt."

"Well, thanks."

Hmm. Marshall or Hollywood? Marshall or Hollywood? Which one will the lovely Phoebe pick?

And his shirt does match her scarf.

I'm just sayin'!

Because I've got to tell you this. I can recognize when some-one's got star quality. I saw it in Seth Haas a couple of years ago and I see it now. Phoebe Foster could be the next big thing.

———————————

It's almost time for lunch break on the set, so I figure it's not going to hurt if I give Phoebe a tour. We walk from Jacob and Luke's, past the Marshall Courthouse, a busy but beautiful yellow structure with a large dome and classical wings on either side. Very grand for this little town.

I like it.

"So tell me about yourself," I say.

"Oh, I'm just from a small town in Delaware. Majored in drama and dance at Towson State in Maryland and have been teaching in high schools for twelve years."

"Did you ever have bigger dreams?"

"I did. But my parents relocated here to Marshall, my dad got sick, and I came to lend a hand. I just never left." *And I know why!* "Though I probably should have."

"Why? I think what you do is great. Believe me, for a girl who hasn't really had much to do with teachers, I really value them."

"I can see your point."

We head down Washington, past the Glamour Shop, past Bare Necessities, and turn into the Design Center. "You ever come in here?" I ask.

"Are you serious? It's the best store in town."

Dee greets me. "It's my long lost friend! Where have you been, honey? We thought you'd be around a lot more."

Hey, I'm wanted!

Nice.

"Just trying to get caught up on schoolwork."

"I see you've already met our drama teacher. Hey, Phoebe."

We chat for a minute or two, and Dee points to the sample foods on display, but since only cookies show themselves, no cheese in sight, I opt out. "Can you take us up to the shoot in the elevator?" I ask.

She gasps. "I'm really not supposed to go up there."

I check my watch. "It's time for lunch break. It'll be okay."

"Are you sure?" Her eyes grow underneath the lenses of her glasses.

People are so awed by filmmakers, so frightened of doing the wrong thing, as if brain surgery is going on up there or something.

"Positive. I'll tell Jeremy I took you hostage and made you do it."

Dee laughs. Phoebe looks scared to death.

Dee ushers us to the freight elevator. We step over the wooden gate and push a button cast in the days of Julius Caesar, if looks are any indication. Then we slowly rise, up to the world of Jeremy.

It's a great location. Really. What was once the local Elks Lodge is now a crumbling parcel of rooms on the third and fourth floor of the next-door building. "Not many people know this is up here," Dee says in a stage whisper.

"Quiet on the set!" someone yells.

She comes to a screeching halt. I do too. Film's expensive.

Karissa Bonano screams, a wild shuffle of bumps and thumps ensue, and then . . . silence. Dunh — dunh — duuuuuuuh.

"Cut!"

I urge the women forward, Dee taking the cue and leading us through several rooms with tall windows, their light diffused by a layer of years without a good clean, through generous archways of walnut woodworking and by green painted plaster falling off the walls. I'll bet Jeremy didn't have to do a thing to create the right mood here.

"Wouldn't this make a great apartment?" I ask.

"Oh, yes!" Dee says. "What a waste."

Phoebe's eyes glow. "I know the owner of this property. Hmm."

Lucky her if she gets to do something with a space like this! Beats an RV any day of the year.

It used to be grand here, I can tell. A double staircase, guarded on either side by built-in benches with cushions so full of dust you'd sneeze for a week if you sat on them, angles up to the main meeting rooms of the Elks. Carved wainscoting accompanies our ascent, defunct lamps perch on all the newel posts. Above us, a painted tin ceiling crumbles slowly, and I ask myself, "How does something this beautiful get into such a state of disrepair?"

God bless the historical preservationists is all I can say. "Somebody could come in here and just rip all this out and sell it, couldn't they?" I ask.

"They sure could," Phoebe says. "But my imagination's going nuts right now. What I could do with a place like this!"

Dee climbs the final step. "You handy?"

"Very."

Karissa Bonano flies by me, blood streaming down her face.

Phoebe and Dee gasp.

I laugh. "Makeup."

"Oh." Phoebe blushes. "I should know that."

"It's okay. It's always a shock."

"Good heavens!" Dee places her hands on her hips, fingers with hot pink nails spread wide. "That's horrible!"

Jeremy walks up. "Good timing, kid, we're breaking for lunch. Who you got with you?"

"This is Phoebe Foster, the drama teacher at Marshall High."

"No kidding? Great. Good to meet you." He shakes her hand. "And I already know Dee. Whatcha got as samples today?"

"Just some ginger cookies."

He turns back to me. "How about I take you three ladies to lunch?"

Like we're about to turn *that* down!

"Sure." I shrug without much excitement. Gotta live up to the title of "teenager."

"I'll meet you across the street at Weisman's in ten."

"Okay. Can I just show Phoebe these rooms?"

"Knock yourself out, kid."

Dee explains these were the main gathering rooms of the Elks. To the left of the steps is the room in which the ladies gathered, a baseball-sized hole carved in the door so they could hear what was going on with the men, I guess.

But the main room, with an arch-covered stage at the far end, complete with blue light bulbs along its front curve, was the stunner of the place: tin ceiling with a large brass chandelier hanging from its middle, marble slabs cemented into the wall bearing the names of the Elks who went to that great lodge in the sky. The list ends in 1944, when I suppose they relocated to newer digs.

"Who'd want to leave this place?" I ask Dee.

"I don't know. Maybe they outgrew it."

Yeah right, because everywhere you turn you meet an Elk.

Everyone's abandoned the set for lunch. My stomach growls. Time for Jeremy to turn on his charm. He'll have these gals melting like wax in no time.

Okay, so maybe not *both* of the women.

Phoebe practically dances on the sidewalk. "I'm sorry Dee has to work, but wow! I never expected this when I woke up this morning."

"I'll bet!"

"Lunch with Jeremy Winger. Do I look okay?"

Poor Jacob. He doesn't have a prayer.

"You look beautiful. Very Grace Kelly."

"Really?"

And maybe poor Phoebe doesn't have a prayer either. Let's hope Jeremy doesn't forget about Joy in the light of this, well, gazelle of a woman.

He really needs to know about Charley's feelings. They'd be the perfect couple.

Oh man.

Jeremy's turning on the charm.

God, if you're listening to me, do not let this woman fall prey to this man! As much as I love Jeremy, Jacob would be far better suited to romance and a life of love.

And while you're at it, don't let Jeremy fall prey to her either.

Seth is coming tomorrow and you can bet your life I haven't gone out of my way to let the Karissa know. But do I need a haircut! After lunch, Phoebe pointed me toward the hair salon in front of the Ginocchio, and the first available appointment was at five thirty. So here I sit, looking like a metallic Medusa because I'm sixteen now; I want highlights.

"Anybody want something from next door?" the other stylist asks, swirling a black comb.

Ginocchio Bar and Grill, by Pepper.

"I'll take a Coke." I reach down to the floor and pick up my backpack. I dig out a five-dollar bill and hand it to her. Charley's been really good about allowances all these years and I'm quite thrifty. Just in case you were wondering where my money comes from.

I enjoy sitting with the ladies, once again explaining the crazy parameters of my life, and if Charley finds out all the people I've been talking to, she'll kill me. My stylist, Gina, is a heavy young woman of seeming Italian descent. Lots of eyeliner, lots of jokes, and there's that Marshall-typical bright lipstick.

Now, sitting under the dryer to accelerate the bleach, I pull out Elaine. Truth is, I'm tired of running from Biker Guy. I'm tired of being scared and sad. I can't really control the sad. But maybe the scared is another thing.

Dear Elaine,

I don't think the Biker Guy is all bad. It's just a hunch. I could never tell that to anybody else. I'm hoping he finds us. Oh, man, how can I even admit that? I hope he finds us. I really do. I just want this all to be over.

There. It's down on paper. I continue writing.

Okay, Elaine, forget all that. I don't want him to find us at all. I don't know who's sent him. But I'm going to find out about that politician and then we'll talk.

———————————

By eight thirty we're done. My hair now skims my chin and twinkles with shards of caramel color. I pay the tab and leave a good tip for Gina. I left the scooter at the TrailMama. The hill's just too much for the poor thing.

I head over to Pepper's for another Coke, thereby ensuring my inability to fall asleep before 2:00 a.m.

Oh, man. There sits Karissa Bonano at a table on the right side of the restaurant, talking on her cell phone. Cillian Murphy's watching one of the TVs hanging in the corner for sports viewing. He's every bit as cute in person. Maybe even more so.

Well, I can't avoid her forever. I push through the door and a brass bell hanging from a cord clangs like a gong. Thanks a lot.

The Karissa looks up and gives me a sour smile. I return the favor, walking up to her table. She pulls the phone down from her ear. "Can I help you?"

"Just wondering how everything went at rehab."

Cillian swivels in his seat. His amazing blue eyes twinkle even in the dim light of Pepper's. "You with the shoot?"

Karissa shakes back her radiant blonde hair. Radiant as in there's so much chemical product on the head, I'll bet she's radioactive. "She's the food stylist's daughter. You haven't seen her much because she's too busy doing homeschool."

Cillian stands and extends his right hand. "Pleasure."

"Thanks." Oh, man. I'm hit with the shies. "I'm just here to get a Coke and then go on back."

"Where you staying?"

Ms. Bed-and-Breakfast-All-to-Myself fills him in on my life in an RV.

"That's excellent! How unusually wonderful."

I look over at the Karissa. What he said.

"Thanks." I reach for a Coke in the cooler and set it by the cash register.

An African American woman, older with gold-rimmed glasses and a slim build, rings it up. "You just come back here anytime, honey." She directs a daggered glare at the Karissa, who is already back to her call.

She's such a wench.

"Take care," Cillian says as I pick up my drink.

"You too."

In the parking lot, I take a cue from Phoebe and practically do a dance.

Okay, so I've still got my heinous crush on Seth. But Cillian Murphy is better looking, and older. And he's really, really nice.

And, oh yeah, really, really married.

Eww. Mini crush over.

I continue the homeward journey. So honestly, the nice part of living the RV life is that home is always where you are.

Hey. A light's on in the deserted rental house where Grace fell on the steps.

Nothing major. Just a dim glow of flashlight intensity. Hmm.

Now if I was smart, I'd stay away. Or maybe not so much smart as cautious.

I climb the cement staircase leading up the hill, up the stone steps to the porch, tiptoe across the wooden planks and peer into the window. Someone's definitely in there.

They've unrolled a sleeping bag in the next room back and are sitting on top, reading a textbook with a flashlight.

It's Grace.

And what is a student from Marshall High doing in a deserted house down by the railroad tracks?

She doesn't need me scaring her. I quickly retreat.

Halfway up the block my cell phone rings.

"Hide."

"What?"

"Scotty, just get off the street! Now!"

The twang in Charley's voice can only mean one thing.

He found us.

Well, Grace, you've got a visitor whether you want one or not.

I run back down the street thinking about my initial brash words to Elaine. *I want him to find me.*

Yeah, sitting in a hair salon in Marshall, Texas, drinking Cokes with Gina. But I changed my mind! I wrote that too!

Now, running down the street in Marshall, Texas, is a different story altogether.

I take the cement steps up the hill two at a time, hop onto the porch and knock on the door. The flashlight clicks off.

I pound some more.

Nothing. Not a sound.

I knock with more insistence.

Still no response.

"Please!" I whisper as loudly as I can. "Open the door. Someone's after me."

Still nothing.

"Please!" Louder this time. "I don't know where else to go."

The street seems to elongate, every tree shadow shifted by the breeze conjuring up Biker Guy. I knock again.

The door opens, just a crack.

"Who is it?"

"It's me. Scotty. Grace, please let me in."

She opens the door and sticks out her face. "Are you okay?"

"I need to come inside. Please."

"Okay." She swings the door open. "But if you tell anybody I'm here, I don't know what I'll do."

"I can keep a secret."

Of course I can. I'm turning into the veritable queen of secrets.

"Come on in." She shuts the door behind me.

"What are you doing here?"

She leads me back to her sleeping bag in the dining room. "You wanna sit down?"

"Sure. Hey, I have a Coke. We can split it. But I gotta text my grandmother first and let her know I'm okay."

Me: I'm safe. Call me when it's okay to come back.

Charley: I'm sending jeremy to pick you up. where are you?

Me: With Grace.

Charley: Whose grace?

Okay, that should be who's Grace, Charley.

Me: I'll explain later. Just give me about thirty minutes okay?

Charley: Fine. where does grace live?

I punch in the street address and basic directions.

Charley: Okay. thirty minutes. don't make him wait.

Yeah right. Like I'd dare do that.

"Okay, they'll be here in thirty minutes to pick me up. So in the meantime, what in the world are you doing here in this house? And why haven't you gotten caught? I saw the light from the street. Wouldn't the police look into something like that?"

"You sure ask a lot of questions."

"Sorry." I flick the top of the Coke can to dispel any sort of possible geyser effect due to my run, then pull open the flip tab. "Here, you take a sip first. You look thirsty. And hungry."

"Well, I only eat at school. Luckily my dad bought me a meal plan at the beginning of the year before he found out—" She stops. "Never mind." She takes a sip.

"No way. You've got to tell me."

She hands me the Coke. "Okay." She lowers herself next to me on the sleeping bag. "I don't know why I'm telling you this. Probably because you don't really care. I'm pregnant."

Whoa.

"I've known since April."

So, what do you say at a time like this? Any kind of follow-up question is extremely personal. Oh well, here goes. "So I'm guessing your dad kicked you out?"

She nods. "Called me all sorts of names, just screamed and screamed at me. It was awful. So I stuffed a duffle full of all the clothes it would hold, grabbed my sleeping bag and pillow, and walked out onto the street." The streetlight shining through the window behind her throws her face into silhouette as she looks to the side, searching the bare wall for the rest of the story.

"You don't have to go on." I really do want to hear the rest, but gossip on a blog is one thing; this is real life for a small-town girl.

"No, it's okay." She runs her fingers back through the top of her straight, dirty-blonde hair. "So he hasn't called the police or anything to report me missing. I'm sure he knows I'm still going to school, because it's not like the office has called to find out why I haven't shown up or anything."

"Why do you still go?"

She screws up her face. "I don't just do school because my father makes me, Scotty. Is that why you do school?"

"Oh, no way! If it was up to my grandmother, I'd have no schooling at all."

"So we're probably more alike than you think."

I lean back on my elbows. "I never said I thought you were different."

"Oh. Yeah."

We all feel so different, don't we? Hiding in our own deserted houses, nothing but a sleeping bag and a duffle full of clothes that don't seem as cool as anyone else's. We eat our lunch with the masses, but it never seems to be enough to keep us full during the dark nights when a flashlight is the only light we have.

"So who's the father? That guy you were with at the football game?"

"Cody? No. I just started dating him in August."

Oh, great. That was not the question to ask.

"I'm not a good girl, Scotty, if you've got to know. My dad knows that. He flipped."

"What about your mom?"

"She doesn't care. She left me and my dad about five years ago, went and lived with some other guy and only sees me when she thinks my father's going to sue for sole custody. Which he never really would. He just threatens that to keep her on her toes."

"Why don't you go live with her?"

"Her boyfriend's the creepiest guy you've ever seen. He's actually a Marilyn Manson impersonator."

I shudder.

"Yeah," she says. "Exactly."

"What are you going to do when you start showing?"

"I don't know. I'm sure going to try and hide it for as long as possible."

"When are you due?"

"I'm not exactly sure. But I think it's sometime in late November or early December."

Wow, I'll be long gone by then.

"So tell me more about you. I'd rather not think about my own life."

"Okay." And I do. But in my mind, the tale has taken on a different hue, reflecting the bright truth that my life isn't nearly as bad as I make it out to be.

I don't tell her the full details about my mom and dad, just that they died. I have to admit, in the brief telling of my life story, and compared to Grace's current predicament, I'm doing fine.

For tonight at least.

"Hey, do you know Miss Foster?" I ask after the tale is told, trying to have something in common. "She comes into the coffee shop where I've been hanging out."

"I love her. She's my drama teacher. She's, like, the only cool teacher in the entire school."

"You in the plays and all?"

"I was. I didn't audition for this one because . . . well, it's in November and by then . . ." She shrugs.

Jeremy pulls up outside in his big old pickup truck. I know this because the vehicle rumbles like a chest cold. "I gotta go."

"Okay. And you promise you won't tell anybody?"

"Yes. But what I don't promise is not to meddle. You need to see a doctor and start making plans."

"I know. I just don't know where to begin."

"I think I do." Yeah, I think I really do. "Tomorrow afternoon, come to our RV. It's on one of the lots on Wellington behind Washington. It's a Trailmaster, the only one there. I'll make you supper and we can do our homework together. At least you'll get two meals tomorrow that way."

She nods. "Okay. That'll be great."

"Cool."

I run down the steps and hop in Jeremy's truck.

"You okay, kid?" he asks.

"I'm definitely fine."

"Make a new friend?"

"Most definitely."

Charley's nostrils look like they're going to split, they're flaring so widely. "You told her where we are?"

"Well, where we *aren't*, obviously. I'd forgotten you'd move the RV." We're about two miles out of town in a parking lot behind a prefab church.

"Scotty, your guard is slipping. We just can't be so frivolous with our whereabouts."

Frivolous with our whereabouts? Whoa, Charley, where did that come from? Been reading good books lately? I like it.

"I'm sorry. She's pregnant and basically homeless. Was I supposed to turn her away?"

I thought of a talk Jesus gave in the book of Matthew about feeding people who need food and giving water to thirsty folks. He'd most definitely approve.

She sighs. "No. I guess not."

"So now she'll be coming to the lot tomorrow after school and I won't be there. Maybe I can just wait for her on the lot."

"No. It won't be safe yet. You can't go back into town."

"Seth will be here tomorrow. Are you telling me I won't be able to meet him?"

"Yes."

I want to scream. She can be so unreasonable. My only friend won't be able to find me, and neither will my new friend. A real teenager from a regular town. This stinks.

"Fine." I change into my pajamas, jump up to my loft and click on my bed lamp. "Fine."

I pick up *Tender Is the Night*. Well, it could be worse. I could be a dashing psychiatrist who's married to a mental patient.

Oh, Scotty. It could always be worse.

Maybe I should give myself a little room to be angry. This isn't situation normal. Not even close.

I awaken during the middle of the night.

What if Charley's right? What if he finds us and there I go? There *we* go. I mean, we may not have the greatest life in the world; it may be the farthest thing from normal I can think of, but it's the only one we've got. And shouldn't I do all I can to protect that?

Besides that, I'm scared. I wish I wasn't. I wish I was strong and fierce. But I just can't help myself.

I close my eyes and Graceland comes to mind in all its shag-carpeted glory, and I remember I felt safe there for some reason. Maybe it's because my mother loved Elvis, my mother loved me tender and true. She rocked me in her arms and sang, "For my darling I love you, and I always will."

Saturday, September 20, 8:00 a.m.

My phone beeps. Text message!
Seth: Wtng 4 pln 2 tke off b thr soon.
Me: Great. Text me when you're near Marshall.
Seth: Wll do.
Me: See ya soon!
Seth: Bye

Four hours later . . .

I quick scribble a note.
Dear Charley,
I can't do this. I can't stay here in this parking lot today. I'm

going into town on my scooter. I'll be at Jacob and Luke's Coffee on Alamo doing school and then I'm coming to the shoot at two when Seth is supposed to arrive. I'm going to meet Grace at the parking lot after school as planned. I hope the danger's off, I really do. I can't let people down because I'm so scared. But really, I'm not thinking I'm in some kind of safe bubble here or anywhere else. Maybe what I'm doing is wrong. Okay, I know it is. But Charley, I just can't live like this.

I love you,
Scotty

Oh! That must be the Whataburger Charley was talking about. A giant orange and white A-frame with a flying W. Well, it looks like a flying W to me. Don't ask me why. I shrink into myself as I hurry past on my scooter. I wore a pair of jeans and a regular old T-shirt. Don't want to stand out today. I really don't. I keep looking behind me. It would be so easy for him to find me. He's obviously here in town. Part of me longs to believe he is a safe person.

Please let him be safe. Please let him not be who we think he is.

I mean, when I actually saw him on the island of Portsmouth this spring, he jumped out at me, but he didn't try to grab me or shoot me. He just said, "Ariana! Ariana, please!"

Yeah, he chased me all the way to the boat. But the way he stood at the end of the dock as we sped away, hands on his knees, catching his breath . . . am I wrong about him?

You can't be, Scotty. He's been chasing you for several years now.

95

You've heard the story. You've heard what Charley said. Just get into town and run for cover. Go to the coffee shop. They won't let anything bad happen there.

The Texas sun warms my face as I will my scooter to go faster. But it won't. It's just a cheap little thing. I hate it. What do people think when they ride past me? Oh, there's a girl on a scooter. There's nothing to report here, folks. Just another teenager in jeans and a T-shirt. But they'd be wrong, I guess.

Wouldn't they? They don't know how frightened I am, that someone is after me and I have precious little idea who he is or where he's from.

The strains of the *Moonlight Sonata* fill my mind, offering a small bit of comfort.

Relief floods me as I enter the coffee shop, leaning my scooter against the wall inside to keep Biker Guy from seeing it if he's driving by.

Yes. Yes.

I collect myself, put on my happy teenager face, and approach the counter.

Jeanne tells me about another cute exchange between Phoebe and Jacob.

I lean forward. "I think we need to get those two together."

There are a lot of reasons for this. For one, we do not want Phoebe taking a shine to Jeremy. For two, they really do seem to like one another. For three, they'd make great foster parents for Grace.

Whoa! That came out of the blue! I almost look around me to see who was whispering in my ear.

But that's it! That's the perfect solution.

Bearing a bowl of muffins, Jacob enters the room. "Hey,

Scotty! Ready for lesson two?"

"Sure. How about Monday?"

"Oh, yeah. It's Saturday, isn't it? All right, then. Monday evening?"

"I'll be here."

He sets down the bowl and heads back to the kitchen.

"He's just so nice," I say.

"I know. What would you like this morning?"

"How about a cappuccino?"

"Perfect." She grabs a cup. "So what's on your plate for today?"

"Just school. I'm going to go on upstairs."

Jeanne whispers, "*She's* upstairs."

"Who?"

"That stuck-up actress."

"Karissa Bonano?" Are you kidding me? And here I had such lovely plans for the day.

"Uh-huh. You should see her. Those jeans are so tight it looks like a tailor sewed them directly onto her body, and she needs to wear a belt because when she bends over . . ." She shivers. "Well, it cracks me up. And not in a good way either."

I feel her pain.

Even more acutely, because here I am in torn jeans and a T-shirt that says, *New Jersey: Guns don't kill people, we do!* Hey, Violette Dillinger sent it to me!

Still.

"Maybe I'll go sit in the other room until she comes down. Will you tell me—"

No. I'm not going to change plans, or chairs, for Karissa Bonano!

"Never mind, I'll head upstairs."

"Good for you." Jeanne sets down my cup, and I pay her for the job well done of waking me up yet further this morning.

I head up the steps, pretty much ready for anything. Might as well meet it head-on. Honestly, I can't believe Charley hasn't texted or called me yet to check up on me.

After plopping my backpack on the wicker ottoman, I sit down in my funky green chair. "Hi, Karissa."

She looks up from her script. "Hi."

Conjure up the most bland, bored greeting you can, because that was it.

"How's the shoot going?"

"Fine. If I can just get my lines memorized."

"Don't let me stop you."

"Thanks."

She looks down and I begin to dig into my backpack because I've got some researching to do. Here's the thing: I'm going to research that political candidate who killed my dad. I've been putting it off since I found out about my father's death last May, but the time has come. I've got to know where this Biker Guy is coming from.

After opening my laptop, I hop onto the Wi-Fi and Google "Maryland Governors." Opening up another tab, I Google "current presidential candidates."

My hands begin to sweat. The Karissas of this world fade into oblivion, and I remember my father, an FBI agent who just wanted to stop corruption. And mother. My mom. Watching his murder.

It's so unfair! They were just trying to do the right thing!

Just breathe, Scotty. Don't get all crazy here in the middle of

Jacob and Luke's.

Man, this connection is slow.

I steal a peek at the Karissa, whose brow is furrowed as she studies her script. I mean, how much can there be to memorize? Isn't it mostly screaming? And appendages disappearing?

And the little timer stops turning.

Okay, here we go. My eyes scan down the list of governors elected soon after my father was killed.

James Robertsman.

Now. I click on the other tab, look down the list of candidates.

James Robertsman.

Sitting back in my seat, I close my eyes and shut the laptop.

My head swirls a little bit and I take a few more deep breaths. Just breathe now. Then get to the next breath. The morning sun warms my hands on the keyboard, the espresso machine burbles and hisses downstairs, somebody presses the keys lightly on the piano, then stops. The front door shuts, the strip of bells clanging the arrival of another customer.

Breathe. Take in the normal, Scotty.

Remember, the Karissa is right over there.

Okay, good. I can do this.

I open my eyes and everything around me looks exactly the same. Remember that.

I lift the lid on the computer once more, Google James Robertsman, and bring up his image.

There he is. Straight dark hair combed in perfection toward his left ear, a substantial nose and a wide mouth guardrailed by deep lines running from nostrils to jowl. He smiles as if he's got all the answers. He smiles as if he's got all the time and money in the world. He smiles as if he's got something he wants to sell. He smiles as if he's got nothing to hide, this man who killed my father.

It's easy enough to find his website.

"A Return to Values."

Well, that's vague enough to sound just right, convincing enough to fool anybody who just looks for a buzzword.

Whose values? Mine? Charley's? Grammie's and Grampie's? Or James Robertsman's?

You tell me.

You smile like you're one of the good guys, James Robertsman, like you're thinking about the good of the common man, about a "better tomorrow." For who? Not my father.

Is it ever right to hate?

That's what I want to know.

———

When I emerge from my funk—because seeing the face of your father's murderer would throw anybody into a funk—the Karissa snores lightly across the room. You know, asleep, she's almost angelic-looking. Almost.

The truth is, as much as I can't stand her, something inside me says she's worthy of true pity. Not the superiority pity, but the kind that makes you realize that underneath the facade is a person who doesn't kid herself.

Anyway.

I'm writing my report on the composer Chopin, the poor sick man, even though it's a Saturday. James Robertsman will still be around when I finish. Guys like that never seem to go away.

What did he think when he saw my father's eyes widen in surprise, then go dark?

I shake my head. No. Not right now.

My phone buzzes. Text message.

Seth: Im almst 2 mrshll.

The Karissa jerks awake and eyes me with suspicion, then disdain.

Are you kidding me? I'm so wounded, Karissa.

Me: Great! The set is on Washington St. above the Design Center. You can't miss it. I'll meet you there.

Seth: Cool. cn't wait 2 c u.

I'm loving that!

Me: Me either. See ya!

Seth: C u!

"You look happy. Did someone win a prize?" Karissa asks.

Now, I'm at a crossroads here. If I tell her now, I can see her squirm and feel very superior in person, that yes, I'm still friends with the fabulous Seth Hot. Yes, he texts me and is coming to Marshall to visit me. (Okay, he wants to see Jeremy and the crew too. But still.)

Or . . .

I can smile like the Mona Lisa and say, "It's nothing you'd be interested in. I mean you are Karissa Bonano, after all," and leave. Of course, the power of that will only be realized when she sees it's Seth I was talking about. And I might not be around when her understanding dawns. I'd hate to miss that.

And there's this to consider.

If I tell her now, it will look like I actually care what she thinks. Which, honestly speaking, I do. But I don't want her to know that. So I take option three and pretend I don't hear her question.

"Whatever," she says softly and picks up her script.

Whatever? Oh, puh-leeze. And how old are you?

"Bye, Jeanne!" I holler as I run through the shop. "See ya later!"

"Wait! You've got to hear this."

Shoot. I turn.

"No." She beckons me with her hand. "Come closer."

I approach the counter and she leans forward and whispers, "I told him. I told Jacob that Phoebe likes him."

Okay, this is good enough news to delay my exit. "What did he say?"

"Just smiled really, that kind of close-lipped cat grin, if you know what I mean."

"Oh, yeah. Way to go."

"Hey, it's not right to have fun at other people's expense, right?"

Uh, right? If that's the case, and I'm not saying it is, my blog would need a major overhaul.

Call me a loser, but I wait outside for Seth. I'm taking a chance with Biker Guy, but I can easily enough slip inside. I should go wait nonchalantly by the set, but I can't. Besides, I don't want to share his arrival with everybody else.

There he is! I'd know the shape of that head anywhere.

He pulls into a space in front of the Design Center in a rented VW Beetle convertible. Black with tan seats.

"Seth!" I yell.

He turns off the engine. "Scotty!" Then jumps up on the seat and out of the car without opening the door.

He looks better than before, if that was possible. His hair is still cropped closely, allowing his clear eyes to shine their bright blue. He's tan too. Will the Nobodies love to hear about this! My blog, by the way, seems to be turning into fan central for both Seth and Violette Dillinger.

Fine by me. The other stars can be so boring. And the really interesting ones keep to themselves and are rarely found on the Hollywood blogs anyway. I mean, when was the last time you heard a scandal about Denzel Washington or Emma Thompson?

He puts his arms around me and hugs me tight. "Hey, my friend." He pulls back. "Do you know you've grown a couple of inches?"

"Really?"

"Yeah, you look great and I love the haircut. Oh, and Steve and Edie say hi and that they're expecting you all to visit sometime on the off chance you're in their area."

"I'd love that."

Steve and Edie are Seth's amazing parents. They like me much better than Karissa Bonano. And last spring they showed me a thing or two about Jesus.

"So, you want to go see the set?"

"I was hoping to take you to lunch first. The rest can wait."

And that includes Karissa, because he has no idea she's over at Jacob and Luke's.

Pepper's mother — that's who the older lady who served me Coke last time turned out to be — sets down small glasses of ice water and two menus. "Would you both like something to drink?" She nods to me. "Coke today for you?"

I love being known!

"Yes, ma'am. I'd love that."

"I'll have the same, please."

When she turns away, Seth grins. He's so cute! "Sneaking the Cokes still, are we? And did you see they have grilled cheese?"

"I did. I'm ordering that. But with double cheese."

"It's so good being with you, your cheese habit and all!"

Genuine delight twinkles in his eyes. Yeah, he's starring with Brad Pitt and is still truly happy about me and my cheese. See why I like him so much?

"You too."

Anybody listening in on this would feel as confused as I do when I try to listen to Robin Williams as himself.

Pepper's mother takes our order. I change my mind and decide to go for the quesadilla and an order of mozzarella sticks. Seth orders the guacamole cheeseburger.

"So." I settle myself comfortably in my chair. "Tell me all about your new life out there."

He laughs. "You were right. Our apartment's crazy bad. But I'm hardly there."

"You're all over the tabloids lately. I mean, in a good way, starring in a Brad Pitt movie and all. Has he been nice?"

It's important to me that people are nice.

"Very cordial. It's not like we're best buds, but he's taken the time to give me some pointers. He's a real pro."

"Cool."

"So it's going well."

"You're obviously not on the party scene or it would be all over the blogs."

"Nah. No time. But we wrap in a month."

"So what's next?" I sip my Coke and make a mental note to remember his schedule for the blog.

"I just signed on for Martin Scorsese's next film."

"No way!" I can't help it. I jump up and circle around to his side of the table, lean down and give him a hug. "That's great!"

"I'm pretty excited."

"So do you like the script?"

"Definitely."

"What's your role?"

"I'm the son of a mortician who's horribly afraid to die."

"Who's afraid to die, you or the mortician?"

"The mortician." He reaches out and grabs a napkin.

"Wow, so your character is bearing the fallout?"

"Pretty much. His dad is obsessed with making his corpses look as lifelike and alive as possible. Spends all night on the bodies."

"Kinda creepy."

"I know. Good script." He sets down the napkin. "Man, it's good to see you."

"So how's Hollywood? Really?"

He shrugs. "I'm keeping an open mind. You're right. There are some really awful people. And it's a peculiar brand of awful if you know what I mean. Like nothing I've ever seen. I mean, so much insecurity posing as exactly the opposite. But with more drama."

I nod, but stay silent. I want him to keep talking.

"So, yeah. It's okay. Like I said, I've been busy."

It's all I can do not to blurt something out. I look at him over the top of my glasses and raise an eyebrow.

"Oh, all right. I'm miserable. And lonely."

"I figured."

"I mean, it's not like I'm really chummy with anybody, and I don't want to become a tabloid freak."

"Good for you. It'll be all right, Seth. Just finish the shoot, get in a little cash, and find a nice place. Maybe outside of LA. You know you can fly in for shoots."

"I'll have to think about it."

But the sheen in his eye tells me he's not through with Tinseltown. And I guess it's okay. I guess we all have to learn life's lessons for ourselves.

Okay, some of us do. There are some people way smarter than that!

We eat our meal, talking about *Green Light* and all the post-production rumors. How it's going to be the hit of Sundance and Cannes and, oh yeah, right. I hope so for Seth and Jeremy, but I'd hate to see that kind of success come the way of Karissa Bonano.

I'm just sayin'.

We discuss my math dilemma and I tell him I'm taking a break to study music appreciation.

"Oh, that's cool, Scotty! I love classical music."

"Really?"

"Oh, yeah."

It's like the clock on the wall goes nuts, because I can talk to Seth like nobody else. It's not like he's got some crush on me or something—he sees me as the teenager I am, and he is twenty now, but he loves me like a little sis. He even said so once.

When the light of day begins to fade, he asks about Grammie and Grampie.

"Oh! I forgot!" I say. "Grampie texted me this morning. We're invited to lunch with them tomorrow! Wanna go?"

"Definitely."

"What are you doing tonight?"

"Going out with Geo."

Jeremy's cinematographer.

"Cool."

And then it hits me. I scrape my watch around my wrist. Six o'clock.

"Oh, no! I missed her! Shoot. I'm such a loser!"

"What's wrong?"

I tell him about Grace without *really* telling him about Grace.

"Let's find her. Is her house nearby?"

"Practically at the other end of the parking lot."

We forgo Seth's Beetle and head up to the house. Uh-oh, he's gonna see the No Trespassing sign.

But I promised Grace I wouldn't tell.

"This house looks deserted, Scotty. Are you sure she lives here?"

"Yeah." We start to climb the steps. "Look Seth, I couldn't tell you everything about her and I'm sorry. She's got issues and I promised I wouldn't tell anybody."

"That's fine. You should keep her secret. I'm not offended."

"Good."

"I mean, you'd keep my secrets, wouldn't you?" Seth asks.

"If you had any."

We reach the top of the stairs, climb onto the porch.

"What makes you think I don't?"

"You've just got that kind of face."

"Guess I won't be getting any complicated bad-boy roles."

"I think you can overcome your disadvantages."

"Man, Scotty, there's no chance of me getting a big head with you around."

"Count on that, actor boy." I peer into the window and take in my breath like I just came up from a deep dive.

"What's wrong?" he asks.

"She's gone. All of her stuff is gone."

Back at Seth's bug I give him a hug. "Have fun with all your adult friends."

"You sure you don't want a ride back to your RV?"

"Positive. I'm going to walk through town and see if I can find Grace."

Take the ride, Scotty! Take the ride! Biker Guy's probably still around.

I wave him off and head down Washington, thinking maybe I'll stop in at Central Perk (how original, right?) in the Weisman building. It doesn't hurt to have coffee options in one's life.

I cross the street and slam on the brakes. Oh, my gosh. He's sitting there. I see him from the side. Biker Guy. Sipping on, I kid you not, an espresso, in a tiny little cup. I turn around and slip around the corner. Where should I go? Weisman's is right across from the shoot. He is utterly onto us.

Oh, man! Help me. What should I do?

Heading up Wellington instead, I veer right on Houston and see a church steeple.

Okay, okay. Church is good.

And churches are open all the time, right? In case people need to find God when they least expect it, right? And they used to be open to provide sanctuary. I need me some sanctuary. Now.

That James Robertsman looks like bad news, just like the kind of man who'd clean up his messes as thoroughly as possible.

By the time I run up the steps of Trinity Episcopal Church, my heart is pounding like a four-ibuprofen headache. I run up to the glass front doors. Locked.

Look back down the sidewalk, nobody coming.

So I sit down on the front steps and pray the Biker Guy doesn't suddenly feel the urge to pray.

My cell phone buzzes in my pocket. I whisk it out.

Charley: Take cover! He's back.

Me: I saw him. I'm safe.

Charley: Where are you?

Me: At Trinity Episcopal.

Charley: Are you inside?

Me: Yes.

Lie. Lie. Lie. But she'll be so worried.

Me: No. Actually. But I'm fine.

"Hey there!"

I look up. Someone named Clarence, according to the embroidered nametag on his gray work shirt, treads up the steps.

"Were you trying to get in?"

I hope that's not a bad thing. "Yes, but the door is locked."

"I'm the sexton. If you'll come around to the side, I'm about to go in. Wanna see the sanctuary?"

"Yes, please." Man, do I. I follow Clarence, texting furiously along the way.

Me: Going in now. I'll wait 'til I hear the all-clear.

Charley: Jeremy will be by in an hour. Crew and I are moving the RV now.

Me: Okay.

You know. This is all starting to be too normal. The franticness today isn't what it used to be. It's all, "Oh just wait a bit and we'll come get you when we're through with work, even though a guy we think is trying to kill us might be around the corner." Life is crazy sometimes, isn't it?

I mean, you watch those disaster movies and think, "Can't these people see what's coming? Why don't they move?" (If it's in the case of, say, Mount St. Helens.) Or, "Come on people, the National Weather Service has given you a hurricane warning. Pack the umbrella and the cooler and ride 'em on out of there!"

So, now I think I get those people a little bit more.

But thank goodness for the heroes in our lives, like Clarence.

He unlocks the door and ushers me into a hallway. We turn right and he pushes open the wooden sanctuary door. His smile, warming his brown skin, warms me too. "The windows in here are pretty special. Maybe you'll find one that speaks to you. Feel free to look around. I need to replace some ceiling tiles and some other things back in one of the classrooms, so you've got some time."

It's obvious he's proud of the place. He hurries back down the hallway.

I walk across the front of the church toward the altar, where a gleaming, golden cross sits on what I guess is the communion table. I've got to be honest: I don't know much about Christianity, just what I've read in Matthew and half of Mark this summer. I know Jesus died so that humankind could be forgiven its sins, but where I fit in I just don't know. And I think it's so much grander than anybody's saying.

In my secret heart, the place even my diary Elaine isn't allowed to go, I pray, but it sounds so lame, nothing like I imagine these people do here on Sunday mornings.

The ceiling soars, wooden with exposed rafters, and brass lights hang down like pendants. Clarence is right, though, the stained-glass windows beckon me to sit. So which windows to sit next to? Beats me. I figure I'll just turn to the left right here.

The church enfolds me.

I slide between two pews and find a seat. The jewel-toned window depicts a green, wave-riddled sea and a man on his knees in the water. There's Jesus, walking on the water. (Aha! Walking on water. I get it!) He's holding a hand out to the man in trouble. In gothic letters beneath the picture the words, "Take courage. It is I. Do not be afraid," shine golden.

Whoa.

I feel my heart, so frightened, slow down as the colors wash across me even though the day is dying outside. And inside me a melody lays itself down, a low hum that moves around through the chambers of my heart. Warm and low. Like Beethoven, only better.

Don't be afraid, Scotty. I'm not going to let anything happen to you.

Oh, wow! I don't hear those words; I just feel them. It's the weirdest thing I've ever felt.

I close my eyes. *Jesus? Can I talk to you? Is that okay?*

I feel that it is. How do I know this? I don't know. But I know it.

Okay Jesus. Take my hand like that guy in the waves and show me whatever it is I'm supposed to see.

And I look over at another window that says, "Receive thy sight. Thy faith hath saved thee."

I don't know what that even means. I pull Elaine out of my backpack and think while I wait for Jeremy.

Dear Elaine,

I have to admit I feel a little blind. I want to see, and when I read about Jesus, I feel like he's a guide, showing me something I should know, was designed to know, but lost track of.

Is that God? I don't know. And why am I writing this to you?

I look up at the cross at the front of the church. This faith ride is hard. There seem to be more questions than answers, and for the first time in my life, I don't have a big fat opinion about it.

Later, Jeremy pulls up in his truck. I hop in, Elaine tucked down deep in my backpack. Spiritual stuff embarrasses me. "Hey, Jeremy."

"Hi, kiddo. Sure wouldn't want to be you right now."

"Charley's that mad?"

He sucks his breath between his teeth. "Yep. You really went out on a limb today."

"She can't keep me cooped up in there. I just won't live like that, Jeremy."

"Rather take your chances?" He throws the truck into drive.

"I guess."

"That's your choice."

"It was pretty stupid."

"I'll get you back to the RV and you and your grandmother can hash it all out."

He's never called her "your grandmother" before.

Now I'm really scared.

He turns onto Highway 80 and we head out of the center of town.

"So tell me, kid, what's up with that drama teacher at the high school? She came by the set again. You think she's itchin' for a part or does she like the old man?"

"Jeremy, you think every woman in the world is in love with you."

The red rays of the setting sun warm the side of his face. "Yeah, I gotta problem with that."

Should I? Should I tell him about Charley?

I picture her, long blonde hair up in a clip as she scrubs our tub or makes me a smoothie. And I know she's stressed about life and that she's done the best she can so far. I know she loves this man. But I also know that one crazy slip of my tongue will dash fifty percent of her work. No. Not now.

"This Phoebe lady seems nice, Jeremy. You'll be moving on. Why don't you just leave this one at that? Do you have a small part she can play?"

"Of course."

"Maybe that'll be enough. Besides"—I lean toward him—"she's really in love with the coffee shop owner."

"Hmm. Coffee shop owner, huh?"

"Don't get all testosterone-I'll-bet-I-can-take-him on me, Jeremy. Let them alone."

"Okay kid. If you say so."

Once upon a time, I wished Jeremy might be my dad. And

that wouldn't be so bad. Maybe he'll be a step-grandfather some-day. Really now? I'd definitely take that!

"Where are we going? This isn't the route back to the prefab church."

"Nope. With that guy still around, Charley thought it would be best to move. So I made arrangements with the owner of Neely's Brown Pig, and he said you could make camp behind their restaurant."

"Neely's Brown *Pig*?"

"It's a barbecue sorta place. If that guy knows anything about your grandmother, it's the last place he'll look."

Definitely.

"So what happened between you and Joy, then? I mean, if you're on the prowl and everything."

Joy was Jeremy's flame at our last shoot. She was way too good for him.

He barks out a laugh. "Neither of us wants a long-distance sort of thing. And honestly, kid, Joy's too good for me."

"True." At least I didn't have to say it out loud.

"She's a nice lady. She doesn't need an old coot like me in her life."

Maybe Jeremy thinks about this stuff more than I give him credit for. Maybe, though, it's not really that Joy's too good for him, she's just not right for him. But that Jeremy can't see what's right smack in front of his eyes, is another example of blindness.

He could do with some Jesus advice and receive a little sight as well.

———————

I take a deep breath and lay my hand on the doorknob. I'm in for it. I know it. Charley's going to be so mad at me for skipping out on her like I did.

Well, it's not like she's going to throw me out on my ear. I might just as well get it over with.

I push.

And there she sits at the dinette, hands folded around a cup of tea. A purple, green, and gold caftan swaddles her body, and everything about her denotes peace and goodness.

Except her eyes.

Those crackling mad eyes glare at me as if I'd taken her makeup and scattered it all over the bathroom. Which I did. Once. When I was four.

"Sit down, Frances Scott."

Oh, man.

Okay, so for one, Charley has never talked to me like that. The fact that I call her Charley and not Grandma can clue you in on her child-rearing philosophy. For two, she's never called me by my first and middle names (actually my faux first and middle names). So, for three, I am in huge trouble.

Of course, I sit down.

"Do you have any idea the danger you put yourself in today, and all for that boy?"

Oh, yeah. Seth.

Now, I wonder. Would I have disobeyed her like that if Seth hadn't been arriving? Probably not.

Wow. I thought I had more to me than that. Going rebellious for a lowly member of the male species. That's not cool. It's so teenagery.

"Charley, look. I can't be a prisoner in this tin can."

"We knew that man was in the area, Scotty! It's not like I was asking you to stick around here without good reason."

"But what if he finds us? I mean really? Is he really out to get us?"

"You know better than to even ask that. How can you even, with what happened to your father?"

"I don't know. I just have this . . . feeling?" I squint my eyes and try to look as cute as I can.

"Yeah, well he's still around. Jeremy saw him. And he's getting bold! Sipping coffee right in front of Weisman's." She takes my hand. "You've got to be more careful, baby."

"Am I grounded?"

"No. But do me a favor and stick close to the camper tomorrow."

"Charley, I've got to do school. I was going to go down to the library at the Ginocchio and write a paper on local history."

She huffs and blows her bangs up. "Okay. But just stay there. Jeremy will send somebody to get us in the morning. Now, please Scotty, do as I ask. All right?"

I just nod.

I mean, nodding isn't the same as a full-on "yes" is it?

So I hop online. I haven't been to the Christian RVers chatroom in a while, and there's the greatest lady on there named Maisie. Maisie. Is that a cute name or what? And she knows a lot about God. I could use some answers right now.

She's there. Well, it's after eight and I think she gets lonely on the road. Maisie plays fiddle at Scottish festivals, Highland games, and anything that needs a fiddle player. The picture on her profile is gorgeous. She's got lots of light brown corkscrew curls, full cheeks, and angel lips, not to mention these blue satin eyes that crinkle from the pressure of a wide smile that says, "Yeah, I can not only take what you dish out but I'll enjoy it too!"

I pop up a private chat window.

LoveChild: Maisie!

FiddleGirl: Hey, friend! What is up with you?

LoveChild: Charley's mad at me, and today I sat in a church and felt something strange, like I'd never felt before.

FiddleGirl: First of all, does Charley deserve to be mad?

LoveChild: Yes. Long story. I don't feel like going into it.

FiddleGirl: And what are your plans tomorrow? To keep doing the same thing?

Thanks, Maisie.

LoveChild: Sort of.

FiddleGirl: That's a yes-or-no question, friend.

LoveChild: Okay, yes. Maybe I should rethink that strategy.

FiddleGirl: You think?

LoveChild: Next subject?

FiddleGirl: One more thing. Did you say you were sorry to Charley?

LoveChild: No! She was coming down so hard. I mean, it wasn't pretty.

FiddleGirl: Scotty . . .

LoveChild: Next subject!

FiddleGirl: ☺ Okay. So then the church thing. What happened there?

LoveChild: I was sitting there looking at the window . . .

Then I tell her what happened. The warm feeling, the voice that wasn't quite a voice, the promise I'd be okay and didn't have to be scared.

FiddleGirl: That was the Holy Spirit speaking to you.

LoveChild: Who's the Holy Spirit?

FiddleGirl: Okay, have you ever heard of the Trinity? The Father, Son, and Holy Ghost?

LoveChild: Yes. So the Holy Spirit is the Holy Ghost?

FiddleGirl: Right. Do me a favor, read Acts chapter two tonight. That'll explain more.

LoveChild: Thanks! I will.

After reading Acts 2, the flame of the Holy Spirit stirring up all kinds of craziness among the disciples, I turn off my bedside light. The light in Charley's compartment shines beneath the door.

"Charley?" I whisper.

The crackle of newspaper shuffles the air as she sets aside her paper. Charley always reads the paper at night. It's one of the few moments I think of her as a full-fledged adult. "Yeah, baby?"

Good. At least she used an endearment.

"Can I come in?"

"Sure."

She's propped herself up with several of her Indian print pillows. Her blonde hair showers out of a clip on the top of her head and her T-shirt tells the real tale: Ask Me Later. "What's up?" She pulls off her reading glasses.

Reading glasses? When did she get those? And am I that out of touch with her?

I sit down next to her, cross my feet at the ankles and realize how much my feet are looking like hers these days. "Nice toe ring."

She wiggles her toes. "Thanks."

"Charley, I'm sorry."

She sets her glasses on top of the newspaper. "Wow."

Okay, so I didn't realize I was so stubborn that an apology from my lips was cause for surprise. "I can't navigate this life well anymore. And you know, tomorrow I was planning on getting out of here early again."

"Scotty!"

"Hey, I'm coming clean."

"Sorry."

"So is there any way we can put our heads together or something? I just can't live the way you want me to. And I don't want to go behind your back all the time, but I feel like I know myself well enough to know I will. I need your help."

Charley sits up, Indian style, and faces me. "Okay. Let's figure something out. I'm willing to give it a try."

That's the thing about Charley. Somehow she knows there are more than two given options in any situation, and she's with you in trying to figure out number three.

Hollywood Nobody: Saturday, September 20

What a day, Nobodies! Was yours as crazy as mine? I sure hope not. In trouble with the madre. But what else is new?

Today's News: Oh, my gosh! <u>Seth</u> Hot, on a break from filming for the next few days, is gallivanting about a large southwestern state. Little Me ain't tellin' which one! Apparently, he's visiting with Jeremy Winger, famed <u>indie</u> director (look for his next movie *Green Light* sometime in the coming year), and reconnecting with friends. Seth was seen in a small café with a teenage girl, laughing it up. Is there something there? Seems like a bit of cradle robbing to me. I'm sure they're just friends.

Also in the news of Sethworld, he's signed on for the next Martin <u>Scorsese</u> film, which takes place in the world of an undertaker. Vintage Scorsese for sure. Good luck, Seth! He's playing with the big boys now.

Today's Rant: Pigeonholing. Once sleazy, always sleazy. Unless you're <u>Angelina Jolie</u>. My advice if you're just starting out? Start out respectable and stick to it. It's like this: no matter how much <u>Madonna</u> reinvents herself, going so far as to write children's books, getting married, having children, she's still relying on crotch shots to rake in the dough. But even I have to admit, I'm totally pulling for her marriage to <u>Guy Ritchie,</u> and the whole adoption thing. Give the woman a break, people.

So, poor Britney and <u>Christina</u> haven't a prayer. Now Christina has the voice to do whatever she wants, but Britney? Honestly, I wonder what her voice really sounds like without all the potty grunts. I couldn't tell you if it's pretty or not. I suspect it is, but we may never know. Violette Dillinger, don't disappoint us! Keep up the good work. Which leads me to . . .

Today's Rave: Speaking of Violette, some of the old-guard pop princesses picked a fight with her, but Violette didn't bite. In the magazine article featuring several pop princesses, one who shall remain nameless claimed Violette didn't really write her own music. Her response? "I don't swing on that playground. Try somebody else." Go, Violette.

Joe Mason joined Violette in New York for a surprise joint performance at a small club on the upper east side. Amazing!

Today's Quote: "I don't think the money people in Hollywood have ever thought I was normal, but I am dedicated to my work and that's what counts." Angelina Jolie

Later!

Sunday, September 21

Jeremy drops me off at Jacob and Luke's. "Don't move from here until Charley comes and picks you up at noon."

"Okay." I lean forward and kiss his scratchy cheek.

"Get on now, kiddo."

"You think you're such a tough guy." Grabbing my backpack, I slide out of the truck. "And stay away from Phoebe. Okay? I've got plans for her."

"Right, kid."

I freeze and stare at him. "Jeremy, do you want to be loved? Like, really loved?"

"Now what got you asking something like that? Do you have it going for Seth like I think you do?"

"Don't sidetrack the question."

"What if I don't want to answer it?"

"Then maybe that tells me the answer."

Jeanne waves to me from the door of the coffee shop. "Come

on in, you're not going to believe what I have to tell you!"

"I'd better go, Jeremy."

He takes off his hat. "Kid, doesn't everybody want to be loved?"

"Yeah, they do, Jeremy. I guess some of us are better at admitting it than others. But what if you already are loved and you just don't know it?"

"Then, I guess that would be the saddest story of all, wouldn't it?"

And I realize I'm not talking about him and Charley. But about me.

Words form in my brain, read this summer, and I don't remember memorizing them. But they're there.

What do you think? If a man owns a hundred sheep, and one of them wanders away, will he not leave the ninety-nine on the hills and go to look for the one that wandered off?

I shut the truck door.

I have loved you with an everlasting love.

I read that too.

Scotty, be not afraid.

Jeanne swings the door wide. "That Banana girl is up there with a young man. And is he cute."

"Seth. It's Seth Haas. Short dark hair? Friendly grin?"

"Yep, that's him."

I follow her to the counter. "I want a cup of coffee with two extra shots."

"Whoa, rough night?"

"Sort of."

She begins to make my drink. "Well, you're not going to believe this. Phoebe and Jacob went out on a date last night."

"No!"

"Yep! Is that great or is that great?"

Good news for sure. Especially considering the Karissa sits upstairs with Seth. In *my* coffee shop. "Has Phoebe come in yet?"

"No. She usually comes in after church on Sunday."

"Okay. I'll probably be gone by then. Will you give her a note for me?" I have got to get in touch with Grace.

"Sure thing." She busies herself with the drink. The Karissa has so taken over my room and Charley'll kill me if I go sit outside on the porch. Guess I'll have to choose another spot.

Oh, no! No way! Not this time either.

Jeanne, who's wearing a plum hoodie with the words, *Seek Justice* on the pocket, slides the coffee my way.

I pay her. "Okay, here we go. Up to face the music."

I've put off the music paper and I have to blog and I like doing it upstairs and so I will. I grip my coffee and start on.

I pretend I don't see them and head to my vintage chair, looking very determined to do my schoolwork. I dig into my bag and see the Bible Grammie gave me. Oh, man. Okay, so if you're listening at all right now, God, help me not to blow it. Honestly, Jesus, if you don't know this already, I stink at situations like this.

"Scotty!"

Are you kidding me? Couldn't he have at least given me a minute to get myself situated? I look up and act slightly surprised by lifting just one eyebrow. "Oh. Well, hey, Seth. Hi, Karissa."

She smirks and he jumps to his feet. "Karissa and I ran into each other last night when I was out with Geo. She told me about her new haunt and I had to come meet her here to see."

So, tumbling over yourself a little bit are we, Seth?

And *her* place? Please! I was definitely here first.

"They've got good coffee." I sit down. "Hey, I've got lots of schoolwork to get done this morning."

"Oh. Yeah. Right, I'm sorry. I know how that is."

I steal a glance at the Karissa, who's smirking more smirkier than before because she thinks I'm pretty weird even though I learn everything all on my own, and Miss Banana could probably never even hope to educate herself like this.

I'm *just* sayin'!

"That's right. Your mom homeschooled you for a little while, didn't she, Seth?"

"Yep. I drove her crazy!"

We laugh that I-understand-completely laugh. So there, Karissa Bonano. "So I've got to get going on my literature paper. I'm reading *Tender Is the Night*."

"My favorite Fitzgerald novel." Seth.

"Really? I'm so loving *Great Gatsby* more."

Karissa huffs and picks up a *People* magazine. The literary irony of the motion doesn't escape either Seth or me. He winks.

"That actress in the book, what's up with her?" he asks.

"I don't know what Dick Diver could possibly see in her." I stare at him. "Do you?"

He shrugs. "Maybe she was more than she seemed outwardly."

"If she was, Fitzgerald doesn't let on. And she had no morals whatsoever. Not really."

The Karissa stands up. "Let's go, Seth."

"Okay. Hey, Scotty, there's a party tonight. Wanna—"

Karissa pulls her handbag onto her shoulder. "I think she's a little young, babe."

Babe?

Even Seth's eyes widen as they look into mine. His face contorts into something that says, "Please don't jump to conclusions."

But I'm going to jump to conclusions. I'm going to jump on conclusions, above conclusions, around conclusions, and into conclusions. She is going to pour it on in the next couple of days. And I thought he came to see me, the creep. "Yeah, I am too young. And those parties are about as intellectually stimulating as a piece of gum."

Karissa starts to say something, then clamps down her mouth. The truth is the truth, baby.

Seth laughs. "You are so right!"

"Hey, I heard from Grammie and Grampie, and they're picking me up for lunch after they go to church. Still wanna come?"

"That would be great."

"That's fine," Karissa says. "I'm working this afternoon anyway."

Seth rolls his eyes.

So good then.

"All right. I'll let them know you're coming. See you at the set around twelve thirty."

The pair leave. And good riddance. I'll do what I can to talk him out of her, but Seth has to save people and Karissa Bonano needs more saving than anybody I've ever seen.

I scribble a note to Grace and run it downstairs for Jeanne to hand off to Phoebe.

———————————

Grammie and Grampie drop us off by the shoot after lunch at Whataburger. Seth charmed them once again. They hug me and I realize how much I'm loved.

I'm so loved!

Even the way Seth's eyes sparkle into mine tell me that, while he's not feelin' *those* feelings, he loves me, one human to another.

And then there's Charley and Jeremy.

Jesus, you too, right? I mean, isn't that what you've been trying to tell me?

Seth lays a hand on my shoulder. "Want to get a cup of coffee?"

"I can't. I have to go right up to the set. Biker Guy was around yesterday."

"Oh, wow."

"Yeah."

"Hey, I'll bring us up a cup and we can talk some more."

Fifteen minutes later we're sitting in the Design Center. It's closed on Sundays but they're giving us access for filming. Too much was going on at the set, and the crew didn't appreciate our presence. Charley said it was okay to hang out down here.

Seth hands me the cup and we sit down on a red sofa, very fifties in design. "So, I know what you're thinking about Karissa."

"Am I right?"

He squints. "Man, Scotty, I don't know. She seems so sorry."

"She is sorry," I mumble.

"Scotty . . ."

Charley breezes by. "I've gotta go. You need to stay right here until Jeremy's finished."

"Where are you going?"

"Celery. We need celery, Jeremy decides on the spur of the

moment." She looks miffed. Good for her. She normally lets Jeremy walk all over her when they're working.

"So back to Karissa. Are you really falling for her schemes, Seth? You know she's just trying to get you back so she can dump you on her own terms."

"Well, thanks a lot, Scotty. It couldn't be my inestimable charm and wittiness?" He raises an eyebrow.

"I'll let you be the judge of that."

He sips his drink. One of those frothy, icy things with whipped cream and chocolate syrup and yick, Seth, how uncool is that? "What if she really is hurting? I mean, you just assume she has no feelings or troubles."

"She's already got her hooks into you, hasn't she?"

"Not really."

But I know that look on his face. "You just can't lie, Seth. So tell me the truth. What *is* it about her?"

He sets his concoction on the coffee table. I pick it back up. I mean, we're in a furniture store. We can't go leaving a bunch of drink rings on their stuff.

"Oh, right." He takes the drink and wipes the ring with the hem of his T-shirt.

I'll bet his apartment looks like the fairgrounds after the circus has gone.

"I mean it. What is it about her that keeps you caring about her? I'm open for any and all truth here."

"I don't know exactly."

"Aaaaah! You are the most frustrating person in the world!"

He laughs. "I know. I just can't put a finger on why I care about her. I just do. Sometimes we don't need a good reason, Scotty."

Oh, good grief. The boy is toast.

"Seth, have you already slept with Karissa?"

"That's a pretty personal question."

"Then I'll take it as a yes."

"You'd be assuming a lot."

"Then give me a straight answer, Seth."

He grabs his drink, mumbles, "I can't do this right now, Scotty," and strides out of the store.

As torn up as I am, I have to say, the big strides with that drink totally do not go together!

He's slept with her. I feel like crying.

So I engulf myself in *Tender Is the Night*. Nicole hasn't found out about Dick's affair with the actress, but she's starting to feel her own boundaries widen, like there's more to life than such a wimpy husband.

But Dick did so much for her.

But he's having an affair!

Why is it that nice people do such rotten things?

Three hours later . . .

Take courage. It is I. Don't be afraid.

The words continue to ring in my ears.

Seth and the Karissa stop by my red couch and invite me to go to the movies with them. The shoot had to be shut down due to something with the camera, the second camera to go down and I think the ghosts of all those dead Elks are telling Jeremy and his bunch to get out of their rundown meeting hall!

It is a total peace offering on Seth's part, and I take it. What he does with the Karissa is on his own head. I'm not going to change him, and if I pulled away right now, he'd only dig in deeper with her. She's just so bad for him.

I text Charley but she doesn't respond. I call her phone, but she doesn't answer.

And the words to that old song, "Should I stay or should I go now?" start running through my head.

Karissa crosses her arms, growing impatient as I try to reach Charley. "Come on! The movie's starting in fifteen minutes."

I feel so lame, having to get permission and all.

Seth kneels down next to me and takes my hand. "Scotty? We've got to go. What're you going to do?"

I think of Maisie, darn her, and all her expectations. And I remember my talk with Charley. This would have been a no-brainer yesterday. "You two have fun. I'll see you later."

"You sure?"

"Yeah. Go ahead."

He stands up. "I'll call you."

They disappear from the shop.

Thanks, Seth. Now I know.

And here I sit alone for having done the right thing. Jesus, you've gotta know this stinks.

Jeremy swings by. "Ready to go back to the RV?"

"Yeah."

The sun sets, throwing the town back into the forties or fifties. I can feel myself slipping into the past.

"Jeremy?" I open the truck door. "Did you have a lot of friends growing up?"

"Nah. Was a loner except for a couple of kids my mom invited over to play every once in a while. It's okay like that."

I figured.

My phone buzzes. Text message!

It's from Grace.

Grace: I'm at this number. Call me when u can.

Me: Give me a few minutes.

I'm in my favorite pajamas. Cotton men's pants and a huge T-shirt that says The Sunshine House down the sleeve. Charley says the place is in Ocean City, Maryland, and teenagers wore them like crazy in the early eighties. Mine is yellow although she assures me they came in all sorts of colors.

In my loft, a glass of orange juice on my shelf and my Bach playing from my computer, I dial Grace's number.

"Hey, Scotty."

"I am so sorry I didn't get there."

"It's okay. I didn't show up either."

Oh. "What happened on your end?"

She sighs into the phone. "Okay, it's like this. I know you're not going to understand. My boyfriend, he"—and she starts to cry.

"It's okay, Grace. You don't have to say anything."

"I do. Scotty, he punched me when I told him about the baby. And when I told him the due date he figured it out. He said I'd better not show up at school again or there'd be more where that came from. I'm scared. So I left the house. I guess you realized that."

Oh, man. Oh, man. This is serious stuff. Life and death stuff. "Where are you?"

"I'm behind the Dumpster at Kroger."

"Come see me. Do you know where Neely's Brown Pig is?"

"Uh-huh."

"Can you get here?"

"Yeah. It's not far. I'll walk over and pray Cody isn't around."

"I'm in the RV parked in the back. You can stay here with us while we're in town."

"Are you sure it's okay?"

"I'm positive."

I am so *not* positive. Charley's going to flip, but what else can I do?

Is this right, Jesus? Honestly?

Take courage.

That's right. Tomorrow's Monday. Biker Guy never comes during the week. But watch: this week it'll be a whole different story.

Monday, September 22

Grace is seven months along in her pregnancy. She's hiding it better than the CIA hides . . . whatever it is they hide. Yeah, I know. I've heard about teenagers hiding their pregnancies all the way up to the end and I thought, "Yeah right." But it happens too often to really think it's impossible.

We stayed up talking until 3:00 a.m. Charley fumed in her

cubicle, but she at least realized she couldn't throw Grace back out on the street.

The situation sounds worse than I thought.

After Cody, the dirt-bag boyfriend, knocked her around (and you should see the bruises on the left side of her face), she went back to make amends with her father (who sounds like another dirt-bag).

And honestly, I think I'm oh-so-knowledgeable about the world because I've met some actors and directors and have seen how stupid and excessive fame can make a person. Man, was I wrong.

I know nothing about real life. Absolutely nothing.

Grace went back home only to find her father had moved out, according to her next-door neighbor, the day before.

We sat in my loft eating a bag of soy chips.

It was all I could find.

"Scotty, I had no idea what to do. I'd missed our meeting time and felt so bad about standing you up."

Man, I hate myself.

"And I was just beside myself."

"I don't blame you."

"So I walked and walked. And finally had to find a place to sleep."

"Where did you go?"

"I stayed in a neighbor's shed."

"Oh man."

"I had my sleeping bag so I was okay."

"I'm glad you texted me. How much longer will you be able to keep your cell phone?"

"As long as my dad pays the bill, which won't be much longer if my guess is right."

It's morning now and we've slept a couple of hours. Charley left early. I know she doesn't know what to say or how to rein me in, but I'm trying to be good; I swear I am.

I make us some oatmeal with brown sugar and Grace practically vacuums out the bowl. Imagine being that hungry and that pregnant.

"Do you want to go to school today?" I ask.

"I have to. Miss Foster is having tryouts for the Christmas show."

Okay, the girl is in denial. She's due to have this baby in November. But I'm not going to say a thing. I just don't have the heart.

"Are you trying out?"

"Duh. I'll be a mother by then. No, I'll do her administrative work for her. Keep track of things on the computer, order supplies over the phone, design the programs and posters."

Oh. About that denial thing . . .

"So you have her phone number?" I ask.

"Sure."

"Maybe she'll get you to school."

"Good idea!" She dials her phone, arranges a ride, then disconnects.

"You need to tell her about all this."

"Scotty, I can't. Not just yet."

"You need to find a place to live."

"I am not going back into foster care."

"Back?"

"Hey, do you have any real milk?"

"No." Soy, soy, soy. "But I have a stash of Coke hidden. Want one?"

"Yes, please."

I pull two cans from out of my clothes bin under the dinette bench, hand her one, and sit back down. "So you were in foster care?"

"Yeah. But then Dad calmed down for a while this summer and I went back home. I met Cody when I was at the Palmer's house. He was their next-door neighbor."

"Can they take you in?" I flip up the tab on the soda can.

"No. She just had baby number four and his mother moved in with them. They've got such a full house, I wouldn't even dream of asking. And I'm trying to stay clear of Cody."

"Why did he beat you up? I mean, wouldn't he just break up with you?"

"Cody's totally irrational. He was very possessive and kinda abusive to begin with. I guess the thought of me with another guy pushed him over the edge. I'm better off without him, but what a rotten way to find out."

"Well, you can stay here as long as you'd like while we're here." I sip my drink. "Are you *really* tight with Phoebe Foster?"

"Very."

"You should confide in her then."

"She's my teacher, Scotty. I just don't want to get all needy on her. She's so busy with the drama program, and her mother is always bugging her on her cell phone."

I've always imagined myself as self-reliant. Grace could teach me a lesson or two. And yet, is self-reliance always the right thing?

"But you like her, right?"

"I really do. It's weird how she's never gotten married. I mean, she's pretty, she's nice, she's talented, and I hear she cooks really good food." Grace sips her Coke.

A knock sounds on the door of the RV.

"That must be her," I say.

"Yeah. So I get out of school around three. Will you be here?"

"I'm not sure. Text me and we'll set up a place to meet."

Grace grabs her backpack and hurries out the door. I stand on the top step and wave to Miss Foster, who bares her Hollywood smile and returns a snappy, friendly wave as if seeing me is the greatest thing ever. When Grace gets in the car, Phoebe gives her a sideways-across-the-console hug and hands her a cup of coffee, from Jacob and Luke's I presume.

Well, no better time than the present to get some schoolwork done. And Jacob's music appreciation paper needs to be written. I took a lot of notes and with a few pictures from the Internet, I make quick work of it. Two hours later, it's finished, printed out, and ready to be delivered. I haven't heard from Seth yet this morning and he's leaving tomorrow for LA. This trip definitely did not turn out the way I'd hoped, thanks to Karissa Bonano.

Karissa nothing, Scotty. Seth chose.

I throw on a pair of jeans, some cowboy boots I found at the Cohen-Shoes-Hi-Style-Fashion-Bare-Necessities second-hand store on Washington, a green T-shirt, brown miniskirt and one of Charley's old embroidered hippie vests. Time to head out.

My cell phone rings. Charley.

I take a deep breath. Here we go.

"Hey, Charley."

"Okay, explain all this, Scotty."

"Good morning to you, too. Where are you?"

"In the kitchen trailer making up a feast that looks as if it's been sitting around for years."

"Yuck."

"Tell me about it. Now tell me more about Grace."

I give her the basic rundown. Keeping it a secret from Seth is one thing, but I've got to tell Charley the truth if Grace is to stay with us.

"Oh, baby. She's in a really bad state. Wow. Boy do I feel for her." Her voice turns soft at the edges. "She must be really scared."

"She is. But she's determined to stay in school and have the baby. I don't know what she's going to do once she gives birth. We'll be gone by then." I tell her my idea about Phoebe and Jacob.

"Baby, that's all well and good, but she needs help now. Has she been to a doctor?"

"Not that I know of. She's been hiding this since day one."

"And her so-called boyfriend isn't any help."

"He's worthless, worse than worthless."

"Well, as dangerous as it could be for us, you did the right thing. I'm not sure how it's going to fit in with our life, but it's okay until we figure out something else."

"You saw her face from his punches."

"She's got to get to a doctor. I'll see if I can convince her of it tonight."

We ring off. Sometimes Charley can be the coolest person in the world.

I head out the door and release my scooter from its prison under the RV. Jesus, this is a crazy time. I mean, there's so much unresolved. The Biker Guy. Seth. And now Grace. What's going on?

Actually, Seth is the least of it. There is that. If he's foolish enough to go hanging around the Karissa, there's not too much I'll be able to do to stop him. Sometimes people have to make their own mistakes and find their own way out of it. Besides, he's got the savior complex, not me.

Time to turn in that paper.

This is kinda cool. Very high-schooly, turning in a paper.

And, wow. I have a friend my own age. Grace and I talked about her problems last night, sure, but we also talked about our favorite music and even though she likes pop and I don't, it was cool. She likes to dip french fries in ice cream too. Maybe we'll do that tonight.

So I handed in my paper to Jacob, who said he'd have the corrections back for me tomorrow. Corrections? What's that all about? I had a cup of coffee and a chat with Jeanne, who said that Phoebe and Jacob have a dinner date scheduled for tonight at his apartment. She's bringing the food and cooking it. And what's that old saying about the way to a man's heart being through his stomach? Go, Phoebe.

And now I'm sitting in the research library at the Ginocchio. I paid the two bucks for the museum tour, a tour about the various wars fought by citizens of Marshall. I saw uniforms from the Spanish-American war, the Civil War, and even some of those crazy, German, spiked helmets from World War I. A telegram telling a mother her son was missing in action in World War II brought tears to my eyes, and the subsequent letter saying he was found and was fine made me want to cheer. I realized how insulated our lives can be from this sort of thing.

Marshall's a pretty cool place. Millions of trains have rumbled through this depot over the years, and this hotel hosted a score of guests. The man at the desk, who honestly looked like he jumped out of the 1880s with his dark hair brushed carefully away from his brow, ice-blue eyes, and a perfectly trimmed beard, said the place was open 24–7 for decades, except for one hour when Franklin Roosevelt passed away.

History just oozes from these walls and the ornate woodwork.

I set my laptop up in the library with a couple of lady volunteers who've already asked their questions about the film shoot and offered me some water. I begin yet another paper on the history of Marshall, Texas, and thankfully, am transported away to a time when trains brought in the multitudes, bag lunches were bought for a song, and the third floor housed women who, to put it mildly, weren't the most respectable gals in town. Boy, have things changed!

But by noon, my real life has crowded in around me again, and Seth is leaving tomorrow and I can't let the Karissa have all the fun. I text him.

Me: Where are you?

Seth: Hey scotty! im on the set. where r u?

Me: At the Ginocchio. Wanna meet for lunch?

Seth: Already ate. srry. wnna meet 4 dnnr ltr on?

Me: Okay. Text me later. Bye.

He already ate. How lame is that?

I head on over to Trinity Episcopal and sit down by a window that says, "How is it that you sought me?"

Well, I don't know, Jesus. I'd say this thing you've been doing with me is all your fault.

A young Jesus is talking to what looks like his parents, and so I dig my Bible out of my backpack to look up the story, but of course, I can't find it.

Jeanne walks in.

"Scotty?"

"Jeanne? What are you doing here?"

"I come in on my lunch break sometime. It's easier to pray here. I don't know why. What are you doing here?" She shoves her hands into her army-green pants.

"I don't know. I feel safe here. I can't explain it."

"Can I sit down?"

"Sure. The windows are beautiful."

"They are. This place sets my mind at ease." Her short hair lays in a windblown confusion that, on her, looks great.

"Me too." I hold up my Bible. "Do you know where that story is found?" I point to the window.

"Not exactly, but I can find it. Or I can tell it to you."

"How about both?"

She laughs. "Okay." Jeanne takes the Bible from the pew and thumbs to the back. A concordance, whatever that is. Oh, okay, a reference section where you can find stuff. My little Bible doesn't have one of those. I like it. She begins to speak.

"So Jesus went up to Jerusalem with his parents to celebrate the Passover, which was a big festival the people of Israel honored every year."

"I saw *The Prince of Egypt*."

"Oh, so you know all about it."

"Well, a little. I'm just sayin' I sort of know what you're talking about."

"Good. Anyway, people traveled in big groups, families and

neighbors from the same village going to Jerusalem together. It was a big deal. And people cared for each other's kids, which makes what I'm about to tell you more believable."

Okay, this sounds good.

"So the party left the city to return home and left Jesus behind."

"What?"

She shakes her head. "I know, I know. But Jesus might have been hanging out with cousins the whole time, and so Mary and Joseph probably thought he'd set out with them, and the aunts and uncles probably figured he went back to his parents. But the truth is, he was at the temple in Jerusalem talking about God to the priests and scribes."

"What are scribes?"

"They wrote stuff down."

Oh. Okay, clearly not a fully acceptable answer, but I want to hear the rest of the story.

"So after a couple of days, everybody realizes Jesus isn't with the group."

"That must have been scary."

"I'm sure. So Mary and Joseph head back to Jerusalem. He was twelve years old at the time, by the way. They found him at the temple and of course asked him why he would do such a thing."

"I know I'd get in trouble."

"Well, sure. So Jesus said, 'Don't you know I've got to be about my Father's business?'"

"That's kind of cheeky."

"Jesus was a bit cheeky."

"Really?"

"Oh, yeah. He pretty much said it like it was."

"I pictured him very polite."

Jeanne snorts. "You can say a lot of things about Jesus. Polite isn't one of them. Have you read the Bible at all, Scotty?"

"Just Matthew and part of Mark. And some Acts."

"Oh, so you know then."

"Guess I just didn't pick that up."

"Read it again. You can read the Gospels a thousand times and not get everything there is to get."

"Obviously."

"I don't think Jesus was like they make him out to be in paintings and a lot of the movies."

"Probably not." I mean, I know how the movies are. They don't even try to be accurate. "I didn't even remember this story. But wasn't Jesus really kind and good? I mean all those healings and all, right?"

"Of course. He just wasn't one to mince words is all."

It's good to have somebody to actually talk to about this stuff. Maisie's nice and all that, but it is the Internet. It's just not the same as face-to-face. Actually, it's not even close.

I tell Jeanne about my experience last spring at the healing service tent revival. The glitzy show, the polished music, the way they made God seem like he was so angry at me he'd be just as glad to send me to hell as he would be to save me. Whatever "saved" means. I mean, you hear that term bandied about, but even the Christians can't nail it down. I followed a thread on the Christian RVers bulletin board on the Internet. Some say it's a prayer you pray, others say to repent, others say it's making Jesus "Lord of your life" and how does somebody do that? If they can't figure out what it really means to follow Christ, how am I supposed to?

Jeanne takes my hand. "Scotty, is Jesus speaking to you?"

I have to admit it. "Yeah. It's weird. I can't even explain it, but suddenly, it's like he's beside me, pointing things out, sending people my way, and giving me this . . . this courage. Charley's so scared all the time. And I am too. But I have to go about my life. I can't wait for people to act like I think they should."

I tell her about Seth.

"And his folks were so nice. They love Jesus, and for the life of me I can't figure out why Seth is so eager to turn his back on all that for the sake of *Holly*wood. Yuck!"

"Okay, first of all, you're not Seth. People have to figure this stuff out in their own way. I'm not justifying what he's doing, Scotty. It's just that if you start casting stones, you'll drive yourself crazy."

Casting stones. Okay, I do remember that story. "Jesus didn't cast stones at that woman."

"Right."

"But he was pretty rude to the Pharisees."

"Right. Which brings us back to the story."

"But my question about the healing service. Do you think all that stuff is a lot of bunk?"

"Some of it. Not all of it. I do know that prayer can make all the difference."

"I've been praying a lot lately. But it doesn't sound so good."

"It does to God."

How can she be so sure of that?

"So anyway, Scotty. Mary and Joseph find him in the temple and he says to them, 'Don't you know I must be about my Father's business?'"

"No apologies or anything?"

"Nope. Not that we know of anyway. But the point is, Scotty, sometimes God calls us to do something nobody's really going to understand. But we've got to do it anyway because we want to obey him. It's all about obedience."

Oh, man. That's what Maisie was telling me when I was going to sneak out on Charley. This stuff is so hard. "I hear you." Boy, do I.

"So do you want me to pray with you?"

"Sure." Truthfully, it feels a little awkward, but I can't think of a good reason to say no, and Jeanne's been so nice to me. There are a lot of nice people here in Marshall.

Jeanne leaves after she prays with me, calling on God to "reveal himself in truth and love" and I'm not sure what that means, exactly. But I like it. And yes, I think it's a little eerie that Jeanne showed up to explain these things just when I needed her to. I even told her that after she said, "Amen."

She waved the comment away. "Oh, Scotty. Read about the Ethiopian in the book of Acts and you'll see this is nothing out of the ordinary. When you follow Jesus, this sort of thing happens all the time. Get used to it."

"Really?"

"I'm not kidding."

"Okay . . ." I shrug. "If you say so."

I sounded like a skeptic. But inside, the thought felt like a space heater in a very chilly room.

So Biker Guy must really be gone. Must have a day job. The thought tickles me, and honestly, if he can only do this on his time off, surely he's not making big bucks to kill us, or whatever it is he wants to do.

I see him in my mind, there on that dock. "Ariana! Please!"

I just can't shake my doubts that he's really all bad. But I can't be stupid. Maybe it's just wishful thinking. Maybe it's because I'm so tired of running and looking over my shoulder.

I decide to head over to the Design Center and avail myself of their delicious samples.

Dee waves from across the showroom floor. "Herbed cream cheese and sesame rounds!"

"Yes!"

"Help yourself, sweetheart! Nice to see you." She turns back to the customer at her counter.

Oh. My. Goodness. This stuff is great. I eat four crackers with a liberal spread of topping, then decide to read up in the mezzanine, where I noticed a very plush chaise lounge with my name all over it a few days ago.

I open up my laptop, check my e-mail. Lots of comments on the blog and to be honest, I'm getting tired of doing this. After a while, writing about people who don't learn their lesson (with the exception of Violette) gets really old. But there is an e-mail from Violette, who says she's taking a vacation in December and wonders if I'd like to go to Belize with her. The blog is exploding with popularity and the contest we ran this summer really gave her a lot of exposure. She wants to thank me and spend some time with me in person. I reply:

"Let me check it out with Charley. I'll get back to you. And thanks, Violette. I hope it works out."

Belize! Yeah, like Charley would really go for that.

My phone buzzes. Text message! From Grace.

Grace: Cody found me at school. I'm on my way to the hospital. I'm bleeding.

Me: I'll meet you there.

Is she going into labor?

Oh man. Oh man. I do a quick search for eight-weeks-premature babies. It's possible they can survive. Highly possible. But the medical bills must be astronomical, and I'm sure Grace doesn't have insurance. This is horrible. Can they get the labor to stop? I have no idea. Wait—I don't even know if she's in labor!

Oh, Jesus, Jesus.

I shove the computer into my backpack and head downstairs.

Dee hurries over, pulling her reading glasses off her nose, her orange lipstick glowing in the sunlight. "What's wrong, Scotty?"

It must be written all over my face. "A friend of mine was just rushed to the hospital. Where is it?"

"It's close. Just go down Washington, around the courthouse and it's a little ways down on your right."

"Thanks!"

Ten minutes later I run into the ER waiting room. I rush up to the desk. "I'm here to see . . . Grace."

I don't even know her last name!

"Relative?"

"I'm her sister." Probably the only sister she's got right now.

"Through those double doors, second bed on the right."

"Thanks!" I can't believe I made it through.

I swing behind the drawn curtain. "Grace."

She lays flat on the bed, Phoebe sitting next to her, holding Grace's hand. "Oh, Scotty!" Grace says.

"What happened?"

"He found me after math, the news is all around the school and everybody knows it can't possibly be his baby. He just started kicking me right there in the hallway. In the stomach. It was awful."

Lying flat, she finally looks pregnant.

"It took two teachers to pull him away," Phoebe says. She stands up and motions to the chair. "I'm so glad you came."

"Me too." Grace.

I sit down. "What are they saying about the bleeding?"

"They don't know yet, but they're saying something about the trauma causing an abrupted placenta."

"What does that mean?"

Phoebe scrapes another chair over next to mine. "It means the placenta is separating from the uterine wall. I still can't believe she is pregnant and I didn't notice it!"

"Grace was good at hiding it."

The left side of Grace's mouth lifts. Suddenly she arches her back, lifting her butt off the bed and cries out, a strangled wail of pain sounding throughout the waiting room.

Phoebe jumps up and rushes away from the bedside. "Somebody's got to do something right now!"

Five minutes later, Grace is wheeled in her bed for an ultrasound, taken behind those mysterious, swinging doors into the inner workings of the hospital.

The conversation with Jeanne twangs in my brain. Prayer.

I open up my laptop and hop online and thank you, Jesus, there's wireless here and a guest log-in.

Prayer.

Prayer.

Prayer.

I Google *pray for miracles.*

Oh, wow. *The Power House of Prayer, 24–7 someone available to pray for you.*

I head out into the lobby and dial the 800 number.

"Power House of Prayer, all things are possible with God."

"Hi. I need prayer."

"What is it, honey? The Lord is waiting to hear your petitions."

"It isn't for me, actually. It's for a friend."

"I see. Go on."

The voice sounds like it belongs to a middle-aged woman with shoulder-length brown hair. Don't ask me about the hair, it's just what I picture.

"My friend. She's only sixteen and she's pregnant, still two months before her due date, but her boyfriend kicked her in the stomach and now she's bleeding and the placenta is pulling away. It's horrible."

"Oh my!"

"She just went back to get an ultrasound. I don't know what to do. I don't even know what to pray for. I just know that's what I'm supposed to do."

"You're right . . . uh . . . what's your name if you don't mind me knowing?"

"Scotty."

"All right, Scotty. What's your friend's name?"

Should I say? "Where are you all located?"

"Tulsa, Oklahoma."

That's a good ways away. The chances of this lady knowing

Grace are slim to none, right?

"Her name's Grace."

"That's a beautiful name. It reminds me of the Lord himself. Gracious from sunup to sundown."

"That's a good thing. Because I think they need some graciousness. If you want to know the truth, Grace needed some graciousness a long time ago."

I'm just sayin'.

"All right, then let's pray. And I'll give her name to the other people here if that's okay. My name's Marjorie, by the way."

"I think that would be a good idea. The more the better, is that right?"

"Yes. The Lord seems to work that way. Are you ready?"

Yes. No. Yes. No. "Yes. Please."

Marjorie begins to pray, pouring out her heart to God, or the Lord, as she calls him, on behalf of perfect strangers. She really cares, or else she's a good actress. But I know acting and this just doesn't seem to be it. Something happens inside me, this feeling of warmth, of rightness. And I fold my own spirit into her words. Joining in with her as best as I can as she prays for Grace, for strength and peace, and for the baby, the "precious little gift of God" to a world that needs more innocence, and I can't help it, I mutter, "Amen to that."

I don't know why, but I ask Marjorie, "Have you ever been to Graceland?"

"Oh honey, I go there every day."

And I know exactly what she means, but I don't know if those big gates will swing open for me, for Grace. For everybody.

An hour later Phoebe rushes out. "Oh, Scotty, it's just what they suspected. They're getting ready to do a C-section or the baby will die. And they're talking about flying the baby to one of the big hospitals in Dallas if need be! They don't have a neonatal ICU here. The hospital is so small. Grace wanted you to know."

"I'm praying. Really hard."

"Listen, go on home. There's no sense in you sitting in this uncomfortable place. I'll call you as soon as I know anything." She whips her cell phone out of her pocket and I recite my number as she programs it in.

I want to stay, but I know I'll drive myself crazy here. "I'll be waiting. And I'll bring you some supper by if you need it."

"You're a doll."

After she disappears, I look around me, lost. Suddenly the Karissas of this world don't matter so much. Seth either, though I hate to say it. At least not right now.

Back at the RV I pace the floor, so much of my life seeming silly and just plain wrong. How wrong? I don't know. It doesn't matter. I feel so weak and without strength.

Oh, Jesus, Jesus, Jesus. You were a little baby once. I mean, according to Maisie, you were God too, are God now, and I don't know how that all works, how it fits together with Grace and the baby and Phoebe and even that scumbucket Cody.

At 6:00 p.m. Phoebe calls. "She had the baby. A little girl."

"How is she?"

"Grace is fine. But the baby is in bad shape. She's going to need surgery. Cody didn't hurt the baby. It's a heart defect. Truthfully, if Grace hadn't gone into labor from Cody's abuse, the baby probably would have died in utero sometime down the road."

Oh, my gosh. I can't even compute this.

"So it's touch and go."

"I'll be right there." I hang up before she can refuse and turn off my phone. I don't want to talk to Seth right now, even if he does take it upon himself to call.

I hop on the scooter and head to the hospital.

Grace lies in a large hospital bed, fear graying her features. "Scotty! Oh Scotty. This is horrible."

"I know. I know."

"What am I going to do if she dies?"

"She's not going to die."

Right, Jesus? She's not going to die.

"Pray for us, Scotty. Please."

"I am praying." Boy, am I praying! I'm doing the best I can, but I know it just can't be enough, can it? "She'll be okay, Grace. What does she look like?"

"Oh, so tiny. But she already has this fleecy cap of brown hair. And her feet, they shook like leaves in the wind as they carried her right by. They're putting her on a respirator, in an incubator. It's just awful. She's laying there all by herself. She's all alone!" Grace begins to cry.

I ease onto the bed and hold her close. And my tears fall too. I'm not much of a crier, but now is clearly not the time to hold back. Oh, Grace!

Phoebe tiptoes into the room and sits down in the guest chair.

An hour later, exhausted from the beating, the surgery, and the strain of the day, Grace falls asleep.

"She'll sleep for a long time," Phoebe says. "I'll keep the vigil tonight."

"But I really can stay."

"No, Scotty. Really, go on home. Your mom will be so worried."

My phone! Oh, no!

Jacob enters the room. "Hey."

"Jacob." Phoebe.

He lays a hand on her shoulder. "I just closed down the shop."

"Thanks for coming."

Okay, well at least this is good.

I turn my phone back on once I'm outside the hospital.

Seth left three messages. Oh well.

Charley left just one message saying she had to work late and don't do anything crazy, baby. Thanks, Charley.

Back at the RV, I pace again. I can't concentrate on anything. I remember Marjorie and think about calling back. Suddenly, I know what I need to do. Jesus sought people right in the temple, didn't he? Maybe I need to pray in person with these people. Surely that would count more with God, wouldn't it?

I Google *Tulsa, Oklahoma*. Three-hundred-and-fifty miles away. I think of Mary and Joseph, too, headed to Jerusalem to honor God, and I realize I have my own pilgrimage to make. Didn't Jeanne say it was all about obedience? I program the Power House of Prayer's number into my phone.

"Jesus, give me strength. Give me courage," I whisper, as I shove clean underwear, deodorant, and two extra shirts into my backpack. "I'm headed to pray with your people. And please don't let them be as weird as those tent-meeting people last spring."

I scribble a note to Charley.

Dear Charley,

I don't expect you to understand what I have to do. But I have to do this. I'm going to go pray for Grace. She had her baby today, and the baby is going to die if I don't do something. I'm headed off to pray with people who really know how. I know prayer's not something you've ever put much stock in, but I have to do this. I'll report back to you through text messages to let you know I'm fine.

I print off the directions to Tulsa, stuff them in the pocket of my jacket and bungee cord my sleeping bag to the seat support of my scooter. Shimmying into my backpack, I start up the small gas engine and ride away, away from Neely's Brown Pig, from the RV, from everything that has ever been familiar.

I figure, at ten miles per hour I can go 160 miles a day. Three hours tonight, all day Tuesday, and I'll be there Wednesday evening.

I sure hope somebody's praying for *me*.

At 11:00 p.m., having passed at least a hundred oil wells pumping away, yes, sir, I'm in Texas and not a bit sleepy. I press forward, thankful September's still mild. I get more gas, and slog back a cup of coffee. The breeze is dark, the road deserted and I'm not sad about that. I'm also thankful my jacket is bright yellow. I really, really don't want to get hit by some semi making time. Or some huge RV.

Grammie and Grampie! They're going to flip. I'm definitely not going to tell them about this. They'll be up here in their Beaver Marquis in a split second. They'll think I'm crazy.

Yet a warmth envelopes me. You see, there are at least five people who'd follow me if they knew where I was going: Charley, Jeremy, Seth, and Grammie and Grampie. That's amazing. I used to be so alone.

But I don't know if they'd understand Jesus is with me.

You are with me, aren't you? I mean, is this the right thing to do?

I hear no answer, but the odd assurance remains.

By 2:00 a.m. the exhaustion bug finally bites me. Time to pull off and get some sleep. I have a big day ahead of me tomorrow. If I make 160 miles as planned, I'll only have 130 the next day. And if I set out early, I'll be in Tulsa for a late dinner.

Gilmer, Texas.

Well, all right, then. Gilmer's good. I turn off onto a narrow road. Old Coffeeville Road. Sounds like just what I need. To my left a small cemetery houses the dead, and oh, Jesus, please keep that baby alive. A caretaker's shed stands in the middle of things and so I set up camp behind the building, unrolling my sleeping bag and burrowing in deep. My scooter rests next to a riding mower covered with a tarp. My Bible lays alongside my stomach.

I turn on my phone. Messages have poured in.

I quick text Charley.

I'm fine. I'll text you tomorrow. Good night.

And I turn off my phone. My eyelids feel so heavy as I descend into not really the sleep of the dead, more of a sleep with the dead.

I must be the biggest fool in the entire state of Texas, if not the entire world.

Tuesday, September 23

With 160 miles to go today, I was hoping to get an early start, and I did. I pass through small towns and pull into a FINA station in Mount Pleasantville for gasoline. I use the ladies' room, down a Coke, a pack of cheese-on-wheat, and continue the journey.

I'm already tired and so many miles remain. My butt is killing me from this little bicycle seat and why didn't Charley let me get the real scooter I've been saving up for these past two years? It would be much better for a journey like this.

I haven't been stopped by any policemen, thank goodness. I keep looking over my shoulder too, which explains the giant crick in my neck. Tonight I should make it to Paris, and I'm getting a hotel room if I can find one. I left my laptop at the RV due to the extra weight and I feel so lost.

I call Phoebe. "What's going on with Grace?"

"Scotty, where are you?"

"I can't tell you."

"Your mother is sick with worry. She's about to call the state troopers."

"She's my grandmother. I've been reporting in to her every couple of hours."

"Scotty, you know that merely lets her know you're alive. It does nothing to tell her you'll be alive five minutes from now. What are you doing? Are you running away?"

"No. I'll be back. I really will."

"Why won't you tell me what you're doing?"

Because it's stupid and it doesn't make any sense? Because I don't know why I'm doing it? Yeah, that's why.

"Tell me about the baby, the surgery."

"They flew her to Dallas last night. It'll happen on Wednesday after they get her stabilized."

Wednesday. Perfect. I'll be at the Power House of Prayer by then, right?

"What about Grace?"

"They took her into surgery this morning to take out her spleen. Cody ruptured it. I don't know when she'll get out, but I'll be taking her to Dallas when she does. I've got a cousin there. We'll stay with him."

"I'll keep checking in. I've got to go."

"You picked a heck of a time to run away."

"I'm not running away!"

"You could have fooled everybody here."

"Then make them see sense. I've got to go." I hang up, turn the phone off, slip it back in my pocket, and wish to high heaven this scooter went faster!

That baby is all alone in Dallas. That's not right. It just isn't. I turn the phone back on and call Grampie and give him the scoop on Grace.

"Okay, I'm on my way to pray somewhere, I can't say where because you'll find me. But somebody's got to go to Dallas and be with the baby. There just don't seem to be enough of us to go around right now."

"Scotty, you've got to get back home. You aren't safe. That man could find you, not to mention a host of other things that might happen to a young girl riding a scooter."

"Grampie. Please. I know it's foolish. And maybe it's the wrong thing. But I've got to do this."

"Why can't you pray in Marshall?"

Uh.

"Scotty, go back home. Charley must be sick."

155

"Go by the RV first and tell her I'm all right. I can take care of myself."

"No you can't. You only think you can, sweetheart."

I'd kinda hoped Grampie would understand.

"Tell us where you are, Scotty, and we'll come and get you and then go on to Dallas."

"No, Grampie."

Why am I being so hardheaded? Did God really tell me to do this? I don't know! I don't know! I just know I can't do this on my own. And now the baby's going to be in surgery. It just keeps getting worse and worse.

"Will you and Grammie go to Dallas or not?"

He hesitates.

"Come on, Grampie! I need you to do this! Please."

"All right, Scotty. All right."

"I've gotta go. 'Bye."

I turn off the phone. Again.

Jesus, give me a sign or something, okay? It seemed so clear and right, and now I'm worrying everybody!

I continue on down the road and it begins to rain. Darn it. I just don't need this right now.

———————

A couple of hours later a car stops. A man in a business suit. "Want a ride?"

"No thanks!"

"Are you sure? C'mon, a girl like you out in the rain on that little thing?"

So I'm impulsive, yes. But I'm not stupid. "I've just got a little ways more to go. Thanks anyway."

"Okay then, sweetie-pie." He pulls back out onto the road.

The next person might not be so nice. Nice. Yeah right. Like that guy was nice.

―――――――

I'm beginning to have my doubts about all this. I mean really. Didn't Jesus send Jeanne my way right there at Trinity in Marshall? I'm totally going against Charley's wishes doing this. And now Grammie and Grampie are worried too.

A small church on the left-hand side of the road catches my eye. White with a red tin roof, its steeple offers up a sort of physical prayer of the people who worship there.

The Church of Jesus's Light and Mercy.

I turn into the gravel parking lot and stop in front of the church sign. "Jesus is with us wherever we are" is arranged in black letters. Okay, when I asked for a sign, I didn't mean a literal sign, Jesus.

Laughter bubbles up inside of me. Well, Jeanne said to expect this stuff! And I remember a verse from my Bible reading. "I am with you always," Jesus said.

But I don't know how to really pray, Jesus. Why would you listen to me? I don't know hardly anything about this stuff.

The red front door opens and a woman waves. "Hello there!"

Her accent is heavily Hispanic and her black, braided hair flows over her shoulder and down past her breasts almost to her stomach.

"Hi!"

"Is there something I can help you with today?"

"I—"

"Why don't you come in from the rain for a while?"

"Okay." I can't argue with that.

"Bring your scooter inside. It's all right."

I follow her into the small church, the doors opening directly into the sanctuary. Metal folding chairs are arranged in a circle around the room. This is different. Not that I've been in a million churches or anything.

"Would you like a hot drink? Tea?"

"A cup of tea would be really nice."

"You just sit and I'll bring you some."

She disappears through a door up at what would normally be the altar of the church. But I can't sit down. My butt is really killing me. So I drift around the perimeter of the room looking at posters displaying encouraging words like "God Cares About You," "Jesus Is Lord!" "Here Comes the Son," "God Is in Control."

Really? I sure hope so. And let Grace see that. Let all of us see that, Jesus. You know? Why are you so obscure?

"Obscure? I just gave you a sign, didn't I, Ariana?"

I whip around. Who said that?

Oh, my goodness. I heard a voice. A real voice. Or was it in my head? I can't tell. It sounded so real.

My arms flare up with goose bumps.

Jesus?

But the room feels empty once again.

Ariana. He used my real name.

My limbs vibrate and I can't breathe deeply. I drop to the floor on my knees as if pushed down by an unseen hand. All I can do is moan the name of Jesus. And I don't feel stupid, or silly, or weird. It's the first time I've ever felt I was doing exactly what I should be doing.

Jesus, oh Jesus.

———————————

How long I've been in this position I don't know. But time has passed in a warm fog, wet tears, and an aching need that was quelled by a feeling of pure love. I can't explain it other than that. I feel a hand upon my shoulder. The lady stands there, tears in her eyes. "Go home," she says, her brown eyes blowing a holy breeze. "Everything you need is right there."

"You're right. I need to go home."

———————————

The rain stopped, and the day warmed while I was in the church. I fold my jacket, dry now, and stuff it in my backpack, and boy, do my shoulders ache! The load is heavy. That lady was right, it's time to go home.

I send out a multiple text to Charley, Seth, Grace, Grampie, and Phoebe.

I'm on my way home.

I read all the text messages that have poured in, listen to my voice mail. I am loved. I am loved.

I call Charley. "I'm sorry."

"Oh, baby! It's so good to hear your voice. Where are you?"

"Still in Texas. I'll probably be home tomorrow afternoon."

"Let Jeremy and me come and get you."

"No. I'll be fine. I've got to come back on my own. Do you know what I mean?"

Silence. She gulps back a cry. "Yeah, baby. I do. But I'd rather come get you."

"Just pray for me."

"I'll try."

"Do it."

"Okay, baby. Okay. It's just been so long."

I'm sure she thinks God stopped listening to her prayers a long time ago.

I hang up, but this time, I keep the phone turned on.

Seth calls as I'm scootering down the road. "Are you okay?"

"Yes. Are you back in Hollywood?"

"Are you kidding me, with you running off like that? Scotty, I'm so sorry. I came to see you and then Karissa . . ."

"Please, Seth. As much as you'd like to think the entire world revolves around you, this had nothing to do with you."

He laughs. "What would I do without you to keep me in my place?"

"Beats me."

"Let me come and get you."

"No, I'm headed home on my own."

"But I'm leaving for LA tonight, then headed out on location tomorrow."

"Text me when you land."

See, it's like this. Do I still like Seth more than I should? Well, yeah. But I can choose whether or not to let that rule my life. I know he still has feelings for the Karissa and I know she'll go back to LA and things will heat up again and Seth, well, he'll have to find his own way back home, like every single one of us do. Like Jeanne says, his way will look much different from mine. But Jesus is everywhere right? We just have to keep looking for his signs.

I can't wait to e-mail my RV chatroom friend Maisie. She's going to flip out!

By my "expert" calculations, I think I can actually make it back to Marshall by 2:00 a.m. if I keep going. My sleeping bag's a soggy mess and so are my clothes. But I'm so sleepy!

I turn into a BP station complete with a McDonald's. I order a large Big Mac combo meal. With a Coke.

I just need to rest a little bit. I pull out my Bible and read while I munch. I go back to the birth of Jesus in the book of Luke and I think about Grace's baby. God took so much care to name his Son Jesus. I wonder what Grace has named her little girl? And names are so important, aren't they? I'm still Ariana in the great space of the universe. I don't even know what that could mean.

After finishing the Coke, I read until the first urge to use the bathroom. I mean, there's no way I'm heading back out with that much Coke inside! Please!

I wash my hands as I finish up, staring at myself in the mirror. Only an idiot would do what I just did, traveling this far on my scooter to say a prayer with someone I've never met.

But that baby, Grace, even my sorry old life . . . something had to give. And my stop in the red-roof church, that beautiful woman with the braid . . . Jesus, do you always show up like this, at the craziest of times and in the oddest of places?

I sure hope so.

I smile at my reflection. I don't feel so lonely as I used to, and not quite as sad, or even as scared. It's not like those feelings have gone away completely. They're still there, but they seem manageable, like I've trusted God with them. You know, sort of like a financial manager. You hand them something you just don't really know what to do with, and they help you take care of it even if all the responsibility doesn't go away.

Coming out of the ladies' room, I round the corner to pass the service counter and stop dead in my tracks.

Oh, my gosh! *Jesus, help! Remember all those brave words about fear just a minute ago in the bathroom? Well, I need you to really take over now!*

Biker Guy stands in line, tattooed arms moving beneath the sleeves of a black T-shirt. His bald head isn't shiny like it was last time I saw him. A fine sprinkle of gray and brown hair sprouts from it.

Take courage. Be not afraid.

The words glow in the stained glass of my mind. But it's not Peter walking on the water toward Jesus, it's me. Can you do it, Scotty? Can you walk on this water?

Okay, so is God telling me to go on up to Biker Guy? I mean, really, I get this feeling he's not dangerous. He's smiling at the counter lady, makes a joke, and they both laugh.

Give me a sign, God. I mean it. You've been pretty good about all of this to me, and I'm trying to be true to Charley, so what'll it be?

Biker Guy pays. "Well, I guess I'd better be about my business."

Wow. The story from the other window at Trinity, Jesus at the temple, rebuking his parents.

Okay, Lord, here goes. I so hope I'm getting the right message from you. As I step forward, my stomach turns complete flips and I feel so sick.

"Be not afraid," the other window said. Okay then.

I walk right up, going for "bold and don't even think about messing with me," and spread my arms. "Here I am."

He practically jumps out of his skin. "Oh, my goodness!"

Now, I don't know about you, but I didn't expect a guy with a million tattoos to say, "Oh, my goodness!"

"You don't want to hurt me, do you?"

He shakes his head. "No, Ariana. I really don't. And I'm the last person in the world who would want to."

"Get your food, Biker Guy, and join me. I'm in that booth over there."

He lays a hand on his stomach. "I don't think I can eat now."

"Okay."

He hurries up and walks beside me to the booth. He smells really good, like leather and grocery-store shampoo.

"Have a seat."

He sits opposite and rubs a hand over his balding head. His face is really pleasant-looking upon inspection, very . . . Irish. Seth would say that, I think.

"Now tell me, Biker Guy, what is going on? What do you want with us?"

"First of all, what are you doing on the road all by yourself? You could get killed or abducted or something."

"That's rich coming from you! You've been scaring me for years."

"I haven't meant to. It's not my purpose at all. All I can say is, you guys are great at eluding me. What is it with Regina?"

"Regina?"

"Your grandmother."

"That's her real name?"

"Yes. Regina Maher."

"What's my name? Other than Ariana."

"Wethington."

"Oh, my gosh. Grammie and Grampie's last name is Wethington!"

"Grammie and Grampie?"

"RVers. They've been around me for several years. Seem to show up every so often. They're on the road a lot. I've even stayed with them before. I'm surprised you don't know about them too."

"There's a lot I don't know. But I'm trying to find out."

"Who sent you, then?"

"Your father."

"He's still *alive*?"

"Yes. Your dad's still alive."

Oh, my goodness!

"Why should I believe you?"

"Because, I'm your dad, Ariana."

He starts to cry, rivers flowing from his clear blue eyes.

"Oh, Jesus. Oh, Jesus." I've been running from my father for three years! "Oh, Jesus."

I run around to his side of the booth, slide in next to him and he embraces me so tightly I fear I won't be able to breathe. But I let him weep. I was just a toddler and we lost each other.

Just a little girl, and that stupid Robertsman came and screwed it all up! But I don't want to think about him. This man, this Biker Guy is my father. My dad!

I breathe him in, nestling into his man-type strength, something I'm so unused to. But I've needed this. I've needed this all my life, a strong man to pick me up and throw me high, to get mad at stupid boys, to tell me guys like Seth need to grow up and aren't worth my grief.

Finally, he sits up straight and blows his nose into a blue bandana. I definitely did not picture my father so . . . gnarled, you know? "You don't look anything like I pictured. I pictured clean-cut and, well, blond for some reason."

"Nope, dark curls like yours. Before I went gray. And thin."

"I just can't believe this."

"I never thought . . . I've been trying for so long. I just—"

"What?"

"I was beginning to give up hope I'd ever be able to really get to you."

"Well, with those calls warning us all the time . . ."

His left brow lifts. "You're getting calls?"

"Yeah. Somebody knows exactly what you're doing." Dad? Do I call him Dad? "You've got a lot to explain. I thought you were dead."

"How much do you know?"

"Okay, I know you were with the FBI or ATF or something, and you were working on exposing some corrupt politician —Robertsman, right? That's who I'm figuring."

His brows raise. "How did you figure that out?"

I tell him the little bit that Charley told me, and my search for the gubernatorial presidential candidates.

"You're a smart kid. I'm not surprised. Your mother was

extremely bright. She loved to read."

Very cool. "I do too."

"Babette . . . well, I'm sorry you didn't know her, Ariana."

"Did she like cheese?" I ask.

"Well enough, but it's my favorite food."

"Me too!"

He smiles and then bursts out in laughter. My dad has a laughter that rings around the restaurant. Everybody looks our way. And it just doesn't matter that they see us. I join in. It's my father! I'm with my father!

"So how do you know where we are all the time?"

"I hack into your computer. You're on satellite. Not exactly high security, Ariana. I've still got friends at the FBI. I've got access to all kinds of records."

"My cell phone?"

"No."

"That's right. It's under Jeremy's name." Speaking of names. "What's your name?"

"George Wethington."

"Okay, so then Grammie and Grampie are really my grandparents?"

"I'm figuring that must be the case. What do they look like?"

I tell him.

"But I didn't know they were my grandparents until just now. They always are just, sort of around. On the road. And they get all misty at the weirdest times. It makes sense."

"I told them to take care of you before I disappeared. That day of the shakedown in Canton — do you know about the shooting?" I nod. "Well, before I went in, I called them. I told them to look out for you, whatever happened."

"They found me a few years ago. Is the mob still after you?"

"No. They left me for dead. My cover was blown. The FBI gave me a new identity—I couldn't even get in touch with my parents—and took me off the case, obviously. I left the Bureau altogether eventually. Robertsman is still in the pocket of the mob, by the way. They thought I died, but it was a setup. Unfortunately he slipped free. When I came back for your mother, a week after the shooting, everything was gone. I had no idea she saw anything."

"Do you think they got to her?"

"It's all I can suppose." His eyes tear over again. "I've gone over that again and again in my mind. I don't know how they knew who she was and where we lived."

"She saw you get shot. Did you know that?"

"No!"

"When you fell to the ground, well, they saw her standing there. She followed you to work that day. She evaded them, called Charley, and told her to keep me until she came back. But she never came back. All the stuff was gone from the house, just like you discovered, and Charley figured the mob got her, too. They tried to burn down our house, but we got out, and it spooked Charley. Then we hit the road. We've been running ever since."

"You all are really hard to track down."

"How did you find us in the first place?"

"A movie. I'm in the security field now, particularly computer systems and such. I was working on a big project out of town, got tired and went to the movies. It was one of Jeremy's movies. I always went to Jeremy's movies because he was friends with Regina. I saw you in a crowd scene. Ariana, I knew that face. You look like me. Well, before I gained forty pounds and hid myself with these tattoos. It was like you called to me from that screen. I mean, a father knows his child. I think it was really that simple. So I went to a shoot of Jeremy's, asked around, and found out you were the child of the food stylist on that shoot. For some reason Regina wasn't working on the shoot I visited."

"She has other friends she works for too."

"Yeah, I've figured that out since. Anyway, I got your aliases, and found you were using a satellite hookup on your RV. I took it from there."

"So who's making the phone calls that warn us?"

"I have no idea, Ariana."

Oh, my gosh! This is my father. I put my arms around his waist and hug him as tightly as I can, gratitude flooding me inside and spilling out the top of my head.

"So, my mother, Babette. What about her?"

"Well, I've been searching for her for years. As much as I don't want to admit this, if she was taken by Robertsman's people, I doubt she's still alive. From what you just told me, she knew too much about Robertsman. And there'd be no reason for them to do anything other than get her out of the way."

I look up at him; his face wears a mask of pain. "You really loved her, didn't you?"

"We had that kind of love not many people get to have."

"Do you think she's dead?"

"Yeah. Something in me died. If she was alive . . ."

"I know," I whisper. "Me too. Oh, Dad!" And I snuggle into his arms and we have ourselves a cry for Babette, and the waste of years gone by. "But maybe. Well, we could be wrong."

"I haven't even dared to hope that."

We surface a couple of minutes later. "So you couldn't track down your parents?"

"No. I tried. But they're not as hooked up technologically speaking as you are. They have a PO box for their bills, but I never connected with them there."

"They're on the road most of the time anyway. They have a cell phone, you know."

"He must be using a prepaid one."

"Why didn't you just come up to Charley and tell her who you are?"

"Because I always just missed you guys. Thanks to whoever it is that's warning you all about me. Man, she's got some kind of system worked out to hide that RV."

"Do you think it's Robertsman who's warning her?"

He shakes his head. "He thinks I'm dead. And he wouldn't warn her, Scotty. He'd want her dead. I'll bet he's forgotten about her by now, though. He'd be cocky enough. Maybe he thought you died in the fire."

"Whoever's calling must think you're from Robertsman."

"That's what I'm figuring."

"Dad, what if Babette is really alive? What if she's the one warning us? What if there's more threat than we realize?"

"I just don't see it, Ariana. I'm pretty keen to this stuff. And if she knew where you were, she'd move heaven and earth to find you."

I'm sure. "For all we know, she's trying to find us too. Unless she thinks we're dead!" That's alarming. "I wonder how Grammie and Grampie found us?"

"Sometimes, Ariana, people just get a lucky break."

"Like we're getting right now?"

"I guess you could call it lucky. But I've been on your trail for years. I'd call it hard work."

True.

"I've got to get home, Dad." Yeah, I'm going to call him Dad right away. I've got a lot of years to make up for.

I can't believe it. *Thank you, thank you, thank you!*

"I'll take you. My truck is right over there." He points to a small black pickup.

"Let's go."

"I think I'll get a cheeseburger first."

I smile into his eyes, and we know each other, because he's my father, and I am his child.

Dad puts my scooter in the back of the truck and we are on our way.

"You need to call your parents, Dad. They need to know you're okay."

He turns onto the road, headed toward Marshall. "Do you really think this is something that should be done over the phone? I mean, I'm blowing my new identity, I might as well make the most of it."

"No. You're right."

"So, Ariana, please tell me. What in the world possessed you to set out to Tulsa on your scooter?"

"How do you—oh, the Google searches."

"Right. If you weren't such an Internet hound, there would have been no way I could have located you all the time. So thanks for that."

I laugh.

"So. Tulsa."

I tell him the entire story: Grace, Marjorie the prayer lady, Jeanne, Phoebe, and Jacob. My talks with Jesus and how I just wanted my prayers to count. Even the experience in the little church. I mean, he's my Dad, and while most kids hide things from their parents, I want him to know every little thing about me. I owe that to myself.

For one, I've never had a father before.

For two, I've only had a father for an hour.

For three, I've got a clean slate. Why mess it up at the beginning?

"My goodness, Ariana. You're an amazing kid."

"Thanks. So do you think my conclusions are right? Jesus really does hear me?"

"I do."

"Dad, do you know anything about Jesus?"

"I try to."

"So do you go to church?"

"When I can. I've been a little busy the past few years."

"I meant to ask you. You normally seem to appear only on the weekends, why is that?"

"I do computer work during the week. I telecommute."

For some reason this tickles me. My dad telecommutes. Thank you, Jesus, at least something is normal around here!

"I'd like to say I have an infinite amount of finances so I could look for you full-time, but I'm a working Joe like everybody else. And Ariana, I knew you were in good hands."

"How? Charley said she was pretty wild."

"I knew you'd be the one to make her grow up."

The six-hour trip ahead of me is reduced to one in my father's little pickup truck. The rain showers down upon us, off and on, and I feel cared for. He tells me he's been living mostly in motels for the past few years while trying to find us. "But when I saw you looking up Tulsa and getting directions to go there, I don't know, Ariana, my instincts told me to follow them too."

"It seemed so random, meeting you there."

"Oh, no. Random? Hardly."

He asks me all sorts of questions about what I'm learning, aware of many of the topics I've researched over the Internet and, well, my dad's highly intelligent. I have no idea how this is all going to fit together. "You know, Ariana, your mother loved Fitzgerald."

"Charley told me." And oh, my gosh! Where will all this leave Charley? "I'd better call Charley to warn her. I mean if she sees me with you and doesn't know you're her son-in-law, there's no telling what she may do."

"Is she still a pacifist?" He raises an eyebrow.

"Yes."

"Well at least there's that."

I speed-dial Charley. "Charley, I'm almost home. I got a ride."

"Scotty! Baby! Do you real—" I hold the phone away from my ear and let my dad listen to her tirade too.

He grins and whispers, "She really loves you."

I nod.

The flow ends abruptly with, "*Well*?"

"Can I explain?"

"You'd better." Whoa, Charley! Getting all parental on me. I like it.

"Okay, I turned around and started back toward Marshall, and stopped to get something to eat at—well, that's not important." Like I'm going to admit to McDonald's at a time like this! "So I went to use the ladies' room and came out, and there was Biker Guy."

Dad laughs. "Don't forget to let me ask you about that."

"What! Did you escape? Man, baby! Are you okay?"

"Yes, Charley. I'm calling you, aren't I?"

"That's true."

"Anyway, I went right up to him and asked him what he wanted with me."

"Scotty, what in the world possessed—"

"Okay, stop. Let me tell you the entire story uninterrupted. I promise you, you'll be glad I did."

She sighs. "Go ahead."

"Anyway, he was shocked to see me, but he was looking for me, knew I was headed to Tulsa—"

"Is that where you were going?"

"Charley!"

"Sorry. Go on."

"He explained everything. Okay, are you sitting down?"

"Yes. I'm having a cup of coffee in Jeremy's trailer. I didn't want to be alone."

Coffee? She really must have been freaking out!

"Charley, the Biker Guy's real name is George Wethington Jr."

Silence.

"Charley, my dad has been trying to find me for the last three years. He's the one bringing me home."

She pauses, then, "Baby, find an excuse to stop and get out of that car right now. Your real father's dead. How do you know he's your father?"

For a split second I feel as if my heart stops. Then I look beside me and see eyes the same color as mine, a nose just like mine, and the same thrill I'm feeling skating all over his face.

I know acting, and this ain't it.

"Ask him something only he'll know. I'll give him the phone."

Dad takes the phone. "Hi, Regina."

I strain to hear her half of the conversation, but no go. Drat.

"Yes, it's really me."

…

"It's a long story."

…

"Of course it sounds like me" — he laughs — "it is me."

…

"Yeah, go ahead and ask."

A greater pause than usual occurs and I see his face twist with pain.

"Ethan Paul was his name."

…

"Seven months into the pregnancy."

…

"Rehobeth, Delaware."

I'm totally confused.

Finally, he says, "A birthmark on his left hand, on that spot where the pointer finger and thumb meet. He was the most beautiful baby I'd ever seen until Ariana was born."

"Who?" I ask. "Who was Ethan Paul?"

Dad lowers the phone from his ear. "Your brother."

Oh, man.

"Your mother suffered a late-term miscarriage."

He lifts the phone. "Regina, it's me."

Charley says something else, something long and flowing and I think she's telling my dad how happy she is that he's alive. Finally, he says, "Yes, I'll get her back home safe and sound. You can count on it." Then, "No, Regina, I don't blame you. You were doing the right thing. Don't ever doubt that."

"Wow," I say as he hands me the phone.

"Tell me about it. She kept you safe, Ariana. She did a great job, considering I really might have been after you."

"She did, didn't she?" And I can't help it. I grin. Charley did what she had to do, and she did it well, until I decided to venture out on my own.

Wednesday, September 24

I wake up and it takes a minute to remember all that happened yesterday.

In one day I got Jesus *and* my father. I think it would be safe to say that yesterday was the best day of my life that I can remember. My father, George Wethington Jr. keeps a little photo album of my early years with him all the time. Now I know I had a lot of other great days too. A long time ago.

Trips to the beach. They loved the beach. Hiking the mountains, Dad carrying me in a backpack, a yellow sunhat on my head. Birthday parties and the obligatory Christmas shot with me wearing a metallic red gift bow on top of my head.

Last night, he and Charley and I sat around the dinette, drinking chocolate soymilk, flipping through pages, laughing, awwwing, and crying.

I turned to Charley. "You know, Charley suits you so much better than Regina."

"It does." She shook her long blonde hair against her back and placed her hand over my dad's.

Around midnight Charley faded, but Dad and I still had hours left in us, for we had years to collect back into our pockets.

My father! He's alive! He's here!

It's morning now. I look down from my bunk and there he is, the dinette bed already returned to a table. He sits with his computer, drinking a cup of coffee.

"Where did you get that coffee?" I ask.

He glances up. Our eyes meet.

So is this what heaven will feel like?

"I went riding around town early. Regina—sorry, *Charley* took me by the shoot and I met Jeremy. Good guy."

My alarm clock reads eleven o'clock. Like that's a big surprise. "I thought he might have been my father once upon a time."

"Really? Why?"

"Well, I thought Charley was my mother. It wasn't until this past spring I found out she was actually my grandmother."

"How'd it come out?" He reaches for the other cup of coffee sitting on the table and hands it up to me.

"Thanks." I take that first, glorious sip. Black coffee. How'd he know? Oh, wait, he was hacking into my computer, and that's just going to have to stop! A daughter needs her privacy. "Remember when you came to Toledo and almost caught up to me on Portsmouth Island?"

"Right. I was *so close*. I don't think I've ever been more discouraged in my entire life."

"Well, they were so freaked, they got me off the island to Grammie and Grampie, who were staying nearby—big coincidence—and when I got back, she told me everything she knew. Which is what I told you at McDonald's. I guess she figured if I thought of her as my mother, I wouldn't always be pining for my real mom. Does the irony of this situation strike you? The very people who love you the most, Dad, were trying to protect me from you."

"I know. A lot of wasted years."

"But it could have been more years! I still can't believe it."

"Me either, Ari, me either."

"Did you used to call me Ari when I was little?"

"All the time."

"I like it."

I drink my coffee, feeling like a big happy orange cat that just ate and wants to sleep in the sunshine. "So, Dad. We've got to get to Dallas. We've got to reunite you with Grammie and Grampie."

"Now that we're back together, I can't think of anything I'd like more than that."

I call Grace. "How are you doing?"

"Fine. I'll be out of here in a couple of days."

"How's the baby?"

"She's out of surgery and in critical condition, but they have high hopes she's going to make it." The relief practically pours out of the phone. "Your grandparents came by" — Grace just assumed I guess — "and told me they were heading to Dallas. I can't tell you how much that means to me. And Grammie is so great. May will be in good hands."

"May? Is that what you named her?"

"Yes. Do you like it?"

"Are you kidding me? It's wonderful! What made you think of that?"

"It's such a hopeful kind of month, don't you think?"

"Definitely. Most definitely."

I give her the quick rundown on my dad. "And we're headed to Dallas right now to reunite with Grammie and Grampie. They have no idea!"

"They've been calling with updates. I won't say a word."

"Want me to come in first to see you?"

"No, Scotty. Go see May and if they let you give her a kiss or something, make it from me."

Dad leaves to gas up the truck while I take a shower and pack some clothes for the trip. We could be gone a little while, and Charley said that's fine. The shoot will be wrapping up in a few days and she'll meet us in Dallas. I call her again, just to make sure it's okay.

"Oh, baby. It really is. I feel free for the first time in years."

I call Seth next and tell him everything that happened on my trip. His voice bursts with joy for me, but something vibrates around the edges.

"You're still in contact with the Karissa, aren't you?"

"Well . . ."

"It's okay, Seth. I'll be praying. I think your parents would approve of that."

"Yeah . . ." he says. "You've got that right."

Dad steps into the TrailMama. "Ready to go?"

"Definitely."

I throw myself into his arms. I just can't help it. He's warm and real and scruffy and tattooed and kinda crazy looking. But he's mine. He's my dad.

———————————

I can't tell you much about the landscape as we travel the two hours to Dallas. I've been staring at him practically the whole time. The way his mouth turns down for a split second before his wide smile spreads across his face. His sleek hands that move the steering wheel in a practiced ease. His warm voice that's so quick to encourage me. He likes to talk as much as I do.

Yesterday was great, but all so unbelievable. Today it's real and fantastic. I'm not an orphan anymore.

I'm not an orphan anymore!

———————————

A mother knows her child no matter what he looks like.

When we walk into the hospital waiting room and Dad says, "Hi, Mom," she turns, the blood draining from her face.

"Georgie?" And she almost faints, slumping into a weak puddle on the seat.

Dad runs over and scoops her into his arms.

Grammie weeps, the tears of a decade-and-a-half stored up and allowed release. The torrent frightens me as if this will be her undoing, as if she'll have a heart attack right there.

Grampie comes running around the corner, sees Grammie in

the arms of a stranger, and looks ready to pound his own son. I rush over. "It's Georgie, Grampie. Your son is back."

Grampie turns gray. "Oh, my. Oh, my."

Dad looks up, lets Grammie continue crying, and I can see the little boy in him. Grampie puts his arms around them both. I watch for a moment.

Go in, Ariana. This is your moment too.

I throw myself against them and am folded into the love, the tears, the joy of my family.

My family!

My family.

———————————

We head down to the cafeteria for some supper.

"Grammie and Grampie let me eat whatever I want."

"I figured Charley was still into health food."

"Grampie grills great steaks."

"I remember."

Grampie beams. "Get whatever you'd like. It's on me."

"Gee, thanks, Dad. You big spender."

Grammie grabs his hand. "Oh, Georgie. Some things really do change. Your father isn't the tight shirt he used to be at all!"

"Billie Jo!" Grampie.

"Well, it's true, dear. You could get more out of a dollar than anyone I'd ever seen."

Dad sets his tray on the metal bars of the cafeteria line. "In that case, I might go whole hog and get the lasagna."

"Me too!" I chime in. "Two kinds of cheese!"

"Three, if you sprinkle on some Parmesan."

I love this man!

This is the thing about family that I've learned today: We are bound together by blood and skin and a shared history even if we don't know all about that history. We melt together like cheese and we know each other . . . because we just do.

And we live in a big house of love God just gave us, and I think I'll call it Graceland.

Sunday, September 28

Charley jumps out of the RV in the hospital parking lot. "Baby!" I run into her skinny embrace. And I feel her fears flow into me. She thinks I won't need her anymore. But she couldn't be more wrong.

I try to impart as much feeling as I can into this hug. And when we pull apart I say, "You're not going to get of rid me easily, Charley."

"Really?"

Dad gives her another hug. "Hey, Regina. How about some lunch?"

"I'd like that."

She's so beautiful.

"Ariana and I were just about to get something to eat."

Ariana.

I mean, Ariana is beautiful, lyrical, poetic, mythical. But Scotty's got an undeniable cool factor.

The decision made, I turn to my dad. "Dad? I know I'm

Ariana to you. But, could you call me Scotty? I've kind of lived into that name."

He nods, then turns to Charley. "You know, I was so pleased you called her what you did. Babette would have loved that. She would have said, 'Now why didn't I think of that in the first place?'"

Charley smiles. "I hoped so."

Fifteen minutes later, we're sitting at a Whataburger. Dad thinks these places are great too. Charley gets a salad.

I take a big bite of my cheeseburger, then suck on the straw of my chocolate shake. Does it get any better than this?

Definitely not.

Okay, but now I've got something big to say. "Guys, I'm about to drop a bomb on you."

Charley stops her fork midair. A cherry tomato rolls off and drops on her plate. "Oh, no."

"What is it . . . Scotty?" Dad's really trying with the name thing. Poor man.

"Okay." I look right at Charley. "We thought Dad was dead, right?"

"Right, baby."

"And he wasn't, right?"

"No, thank goodness." Dad.

"Okay, this is going to sound crazy. But—" I sip Charley's water. "I don't think we should give up on my mother. She might be alive too."

Dad nods. "I've been thinking the same thing."

"Me too," Charley says.

"And if she is, she's probably all alone thinking we're all dead. Can you imagine how horrible it is for her if she's still alive?"

"No, baby, I can't." Charley looks at my dad. "What do you

say, George? Join us in the RV? Call in some more of your FBI favors?"

"Yes. This is good. I can still work from the road."

Charley's eyes sparkle. "If she's alive, we can find her together."

"Imagine her face when she sees us!" I cry. Then look around. Okay, that was too loud.

"Oh, Ari—Scotty, don't get your hopes up, honey." Dad places his hand over Charley's. "You sure about this? I mean, she may have a whole new life, or we might find that—"

"I'd rather know the truth, George. It's time for that, you know?"

"I do," he says.

"I do too. When do we get started, Dad?"

"Well, I was thinking we could head back to Maryland, go to the beach for a couple of weeks. It's nice there in the fall. And then we can begin the search in earnest."

Excitement and anxiety zing through my veins. Yes, this is right.

Back on the road we'll go.

But then, I don't know any other way.

"You know, Charley, we still don't know who's been warning us with those phone calls."

"Maybe not, but I know he won't be warning us again." Dad.

"How do you know?" Charley.

"Well, I figured there must be some sort of tracing mechanism in my stuff. So I searched my truck—found nothing. And then I cut apart the lining of my leather jacket. Sure enough, there it was, sewn in the lining."

"I was wondering why the calls stopped." Charley.

"I threw it into the Dumpster at the Brown Pig."

For some reason, we all find this extremely funny.

Sunday, October 12

Grammie and Grampie came to the beach too. We're camped out in Ocean City, in an RV park called Montego Bay. The chill wind whips the pages on my book. I'm almost finished with *Tender Is the Night*. Dad says it was Mom's favorite Fitzgerald novel. But I'll be honest. I still like *The Great Gatsby* better. Maybe Babette and I will be able to discuss why sometime in the future. Hopefully the near future.

Dick Diver doesn't end up with that awful actress and I'm so glad about that!

My cell phone rings.

Grace.

"I'm still in Dallas. You'll never believe what's happened, Scotty!"

"How's May?"

"Great! I'll be able to take her home next week! She's breathing on her own, gaining weight."

"Where will home be, Grace?"

"I'll be living with Phoebe! Isn't that great?"

I knew it! I knew it!

"Yes! Definitely. I'm so happy for you, Grace."

"Scotty, I don't know what I would have done without you."

"No, Grace. God was looking out for you."

"You know what? I believe that. I really do."

We chat for another fifteen minutes or so, talking about the restraining order against Cody, daycare, and the cute outfits Jacob bought for the baby, then ring off. Phoebe's taking on a lot of responsibility. But she can handle it. And I don't know why I felt I had to get Jacob painted into the picture. But hopefully he'll continue loving Phoebe. We all need as many people to love us as we can get.

Grammie whirls in my direction, her caftan blowing in the autumn breeze. "Scotty! It's time for lunch! Grampie grilled steaks for you and your father, chicken breasts for us" — they've started watching their cholesterol — "and portobello mushrooms for Charley."

"Sounds like a feast." I rise and fold up my beach chair.

"Oh, it is, dear. It surely is."

One place is missing at our table, though, and we are all aware of it, despite the joy that hasn't yet worn off.

But we'll find her.

Babette, if you're out there, get ready, because we are coming your way.

lisa samson

book 3

Romancing
Hollywood
Nobody

a novel

THiNK

Sample from

Romancing Hollywood Nobody

Monday, April 30, 6:00 a.m.

My eyes open. Yes, yes, yes. The greatest man in the entire world is brewing coffee right here in the TrailMama.

"Dad."

"Morning, Scotty. The big day."

"Yep."

"And this time, you won't have to drive."

I throw back the covers on my loft bed and slip down to the dinette of our RV. My dad sleeps on the dinette bed. He's usually got it turned back into our kitchen table by 5:00 a.m. What can I say? The guy may be just as much in love with cheese as I am, but honestly? Our body clocks are about as different as Liam Neeson and Seth Green.

You know what I mean?

And we have lots of differences.

For one, he's totally a nonfiction person and I'm fiction all the way. For two, he has no fashion sense whatsoever. And for three, he has way more hope for people at the outset than I do. Man, do I have a lot to learn on that front.

He hands me a mug and I sip the dark liquid. I was roasting coffee beans for a while there, but Dad took the mantle upon himself and he does a better job.

Starbucks Schmarbucks.

He hands me another mug and I head to the back of the TrailMama to wake up Charley. My grandmother looks so sweet in the morning, her frosted, silver-blond hair fanned out on the pillow. You know, she could pass for an aging mermaid. A really short one, true.

I wave the mug as close as I can to her nose without fear of her rearing up, knocking the mug and burning her face. "Charley . . ." I singsong. "Time to get a move on. Time to get back on the road."

And boy is this a switch!

All I can say is, your life can be going one way for years and years and then, snap-snap-snap-in-a-Z, it looks like it had major plastic surgery.

Only in reverse. Imagine life just getting more and more real. I like it.

Charley opens her eyes. "Hey, baby. You brought me coffee. You get groovier every day."

She's a hippie. What can I say?

And she started drinking coffee again when I ran away last fall in Texas. I mean, I didn't really run away. I went somewhere with a perfectly good reason for not telling anyone, and I was planning to return as soon as my mission was done.

She scootches up to a sitting position, hair still in a cloud, takes the mug and, with that dazzling smile still on her face (think Kate Hudson) sips the coffee. She sighs.

"I know," I say. "How did we make it so long without him?"

"Now that he's with us, I don't know. But somehow we did, didn't we, baby? It may not have always been graceful and smooth, but we made it together."

I rub her shoulder. "Yeah. I guess you could say we pretty much did."

The engine hums its movin'-on song. "Dad's ready to pull out. Let's hit it."

"Scotland, here we come."

Scotland? Well, sort of.

About the Author

Lisa Samson is the author of twenty books, including the Christy Award-winning *Songbird*. *Hollywood Nobody* was her first Young Adult book. She speaks at various writers' conferences throughout the year. Lisa and her husband, Will, reside in Kentucky with their three children. Learn more about Lisa at www.lisasamson .com.

Check out these other great titles from NavPress TH1NK!

lisa samson

Hollywood Nobody
Lisa Samson
ISBN-13: 9781-60006-091-5
ISBN-10: 1-60006-091-9

Fifteen-year-old Scotty Dawn has spent her young life on the road, traveling to movie sets with her single mom, Charley, a food designer. Complicating matters is a mother who offers no guidance and a father she's never met. Now Scotty is determined to discover what she wants from life. The first in a series, *Hollywood Nobody* is a novel for teen girls that examines real issues with honesty and humor.

The Big Picture
Jenny B. Jones
ISBN-13: 978-1-60006-208-7
ISBN-10: 1-60006-208-3

Katie Parker is having a bad day. Not only was she dumped by her boyfriend for his ex at the Big Picture drive-in, Katie arrives at her foster home, where a surprise guest is waiting. A KATIE PARKER PRODUCTION series offers teen girls real-world fiction balanced by hope and humor. Don't miss the first two in the series, *In Between* and *On the Loose*.

My Beautiful Disaster
Michelle Buckman
ISBN-13: 978-1-60006-083-0
ISBN-10: 1-60006-083-8

Dixie Chambers is an average high school girl who's just been granted access into the popular crowd. Dixie falls into an intimate relationship with a local rock star. But as his nice-guy facade begins to slip, Dixie learns that she's pregnant. Terrified of her family's response, she faces a tough decision that will change her life forever. Author Michelle Buckman balances tough themes with the hope found in God alone. *My Beautiful Disaster* is the latest release in THE PATHWAY COLLECTION.

To order copies, visit your local Christian bookstore, call NavPress at 1-800-366-7788, or log on to www.navpress.com.
To locate a Christian bookstore near you, call 1-800-991-7747.